Hope for the Morrow

Hope for the Morrow

Book Four
of the Enduring Faith Series

SUSAN C. FELDHAKE

ZondervanPublishingHouse
Grand Rapids, Michigan
A Division of HarperCollinsPublishers

Hope for the Morrow
Copyright © 1993 by Susan C. Feldhake

Requests for information should be addressed to:
Zondervan Publishing House
Grand Rapids, Michigan 49530

Library of Congress Cataloging in Publication Data

Feldhake, Susan C.
   Hope for the Morrow / Susan C. Feldhake
      p.   cm. – (Enduring faith series : bk. 4)
   ISBN 0-310-48141-4 (paper)
  I. Title. II. Series: Feldhake, Susan C. Enduring faith series : bk. 4.
  PS3556.E4575H66   1993
  813'.54—dc20   92-36314
                                                        CIP

Edited by Anne Severance
Cover design by Jody Langley
Cover illustration by Jim Spoelstra

Printed in the United States of America

93 94 95 96 97 98 99 00 01 / LP / 10 9 8 7 6 5 4 3 2 1

For Robert A. and Agnes F. Feldhake,
Louisville, Illinois,
their sons and daughters,
and generations of area people
who are my husband's kin
but have become my cherished loved ones as well

Prologue

AT THE BANTY rooster's crow, heralding dawn's arrival, Lizzie Stone flicked her eyes open. In the bed beside her, her daughter Harmony was still sleeping.

Lizzie was plumb weary from her labors of the day before, but there would be no lying abed for a woman with a busy household. She worked hard and long on her farm, but her four children had always worked alongside her with nary a complaint. Now, despite the trials of the past years, one had only to look about her well-tended acreage to see that all had been put right again.

As Lizzie buttoned her simple calico housedress, her eyes fell on the framed sampler she'd embroidered when she was but a little girl at her mama's knee, bless Fanny Preston's soul:

THIS IS THE DAY THE LORD HATH MADE. REJOICE AND BE GLAD IN IT.

Even when the days had been darkest, Lizzie had hung onto her hope, and she felt a surge of thanksgiving for the hand of Providence that had sustained her family and neighbors in the Salt Creek community just as the Good Book had strengthened those who had gone on before.

Mentally, Lizzie ticked off a roll call of the dear departed: There was Sue Ellen Wheeler, who'd borne the twins, Molly and Marissa, smiling with hope even as her life's blood ebbed from her body.

There was Tom McPherson. Lizzie had heard Pa Wheeler speak of him so often that it was almost as if she, too, had known the young Christian from Fayette County who'd given his life in a mining accident in the hope that Alton Wheeler would live to find new life in the Lord.

And there was Harmon Childers, Lizzie's first husband and first love, who had been so filled with hope—a hope she'd shared—when they pledged their wedding vows that long ago day. Their future was bright with promise when Harm was taken in the midst of his labors as he worked to make their dreams come true.

Ah, the events experienced, the tragedies endured . . . why, sometimes it was enough to make a body dizzy! She thought of the day Pa died, followed so quickly by Ma's untimely passing—then Jeremiah's freakish accident with the mule that had robbed Lizzie of her second husband's companionship, leaving him with the mind of a child.

As if that hadn't been enough, in the face of all that had happened, she had had to reckon with her brother's fury as he left the faith of his childhood to follow a wayward path. Now only the Good Lord knew Rory Preston's whereabouts! And adding insult to injury, before his hasty departure, Rory had sold their parents' farmstead, depriving Lizzie of her rightful inheritance. Still, the new owner, Brad Mathews, and his darling girls had turned out to be not a bane but a blessing. In fact, it was Brad and his family who kept Lizzie's hope alive!

She'd have to be a liar, though, Lizzie mused, if she didn't confess that there had been many a time when her faith had been sorely tested and it had been difficult to face the new day and be glad. Nights when she'd cried herself to sleep. Mornings when she had awakened with a heavy heart. Days when her head purely swam from prayers that, it appeared to her, the Lord was taking His own sweet time in answering.

In those dark moments it would have been so easy to give up hope, as Rory had done. And she would have, too, if it hadn't been for a faith that held her steady though the floodwaters raged about her and the fires swept over her. But Lizzie hung on, clinging to the hope that someday she'd put down her earthly burdens and go to her eternal home in heaven where she'd receive her reward for faithfulness and be reunited with the loved ones who had gone on before.

Outside, the rooster's insistent crowing stirred the sleepy Central Illinois farmstead to life and action. Pigs grunted and rooted in their wallow. Hens scratched about, encouraging newly hatched chicks to peck for a stray kernel of corn in the dust of the farmyard. Mules brayed. A horse whinnied. And a mourning dove added his plaintive lament from a nearby fencepost.

The barnyard chorus awakened Lizzie's two older sons, Lester and Maylon, now responsible young men under the tutelage of Pa Wheeler and Brad Mathews. They thumped out of their attic beds and proceeded down the rickety ladder without having to be summoned from their rest.

Lizzie sighed as she slowly walked into the kitchen. Donning her apron, she stirred the ashes in the cookstove, causing the slumbering fire to flare up—the way, she decided, a person's very soul, stirred 'round and 'round by the events of life, could make faith flame anew.

Today there might be fresh concerns to confront, she realized, as she ground coffee beans to brew in time for breakfast. Today there might be sorrows to blight happiness. Today there might be losses to bear. But always, always, come what may, she could endure if she carried within her heart, hope for all of their tomorrows!

chapter
1

SUMMER WORE on like a calico dress that has seen too many washdays, and as July dragged to a close, so did the prime blackberry harvest season.

Lizzie and her children had picked and sold enough berries to pay the taxes on the farm and even put by a little cash for an emergency. After the necessities were provided, they had gathered berries for Lizzie to preserve into jams, jellies, sauces, fruit leathers, and delectable cobblers, which she would serve swimming in sweet cream from the top milk given by the family's brown Swiss cow, Della.

Hating to let any of the year's bumper crop of blackberries go to waste, if only out of habit, Lizzie found herself carrying a tin lard pail to a thicket near the cabin.

Picking was sparse, but after half an hour out in the noonday sun, while the boys performed chores around the farm and Harmony remained in the shelter of the cabin, Lizzie had gathered enough fruit for blackberry dumplings for an after-supper treat.

She took a moment to rest, putting one hand to the small of her aching back, and stretched. Gazing at her neat farmstead, she found it hard to recall a time when all this— rolling acres of pastureland, snug cabin, barn, henhouse, pigpen, and garden plot—had once been only untamed wilderness. Here she and her first husband, Harmon Childers, had started their lives together. Diligently they had turned their hands to carving out a place for themselves on this Union Township parcel of land on the banks of Salt Creek.

Twelve miles to the north was Effingham, the county seat, where records for Lizzie's marriage to Jeremiah Stone were also filed, as had the fact of Harm's passing been duly recorded.

Strange, how those few facts, neatly scripted and entered into bound ledgers, could chronicle so much of the heartache and hope of her earlier years, Lizzie mused. Yet so much more was written on the fleshy tablets of her heart—the accident that had left Jem more child than husband—the bitter encounter that had sent her brother, Rory, fleeing in pursuit of some worldly dream—the kind neighbor whose chaste love sustained her now—

"Lizzie! Yoo-hoo, Lizzie!" came a faint voice interrupting her reverie.

Clutching her bucket, Lizzie craned her neck and shielded her eyes with one hand. Then self-consciously, she removed her bonnet and raked her hand through her hair, tangled now and tumbling from the knot at the back of her neck.

"Lizzie! Oh, Liz—zie!"

Spotting her pa-in-law's horses by the front gate, Lizzie left the brier patch and hurried toward the caller, untwisting her long skirt that had been pulled up and tied over her petticoat to admit any cooling breeze.

Sensing her approach, the huge pair of Clydesdales stomped their feet, switched their tails to ward off the pesky flies, and snorted as they pawed the hard ground impatiently, awaiting a refreshing bucket of water.

"Over here, Miss Abby!" called Lizzie, waving her bonnet. "I'm a-comin' to the house! Be there directly!"

Miss Abby waved in acknowledgment, then seated herself in the shade of an oak tree on a bench that Jeremiah had constructed before his accident.

Even though Lizzie was tired—bone tired—her heart was light and her feet took wings in anticipation of a pleasant visit with Abigail Wheeler, her father-in-law's young wife. As she walked, she rehearsed the refreshments she would serve her guest—lemonade with a sprig of mint and some of those good sugar cookies she'd baked this morning. It would be fine to sit a spell and enjoy a bit of conversation with another woman who shared her common hopes and concerns.

Lizzie gave Abby a wide smile, fanned her reddened face with her bonnet, and extended the berries for the Salt Creek community schoolmarm's admiration.

"Help yourself," Lizzie invited as the younger woman plucked a few plump berries from the bucket and popped them in her mouth. "Blackberries are few 'n' far between at this time o' year, but just like the last rose o' summer always seems to smell the sweetest, I think these stragglers taste the best, don't you?"

Without waiting for an answer, Lizzie excused herself to take the remaining berries into the house, where she set Harmony to rinsing and cleaning the fruit. She returned within minutes with a pitcher of fresh lemonade and two glasses filled with ice chipped from the block in the icebox. Ice was a treat, but one she felt she'd more than earned as a result of the summer's hard labor.

"My, but the days have slipped away fast," Lizzie said, seating herself beside Abby and offering her a cookie. "How've you been?"

The schoolteacher accepted the refreshments and gave Lizzie a coy smile, her eyes twinkling.

"As a matter of fact, I couldn't be better. No, couldn't be better," she repeated, her voice slightly tremulous. "Just this very day, I paid a visit to a physician in town—"

A shadow seemed to dim the sparkle in Miss Abby's blue eyes, and she hesitated as if uncertain whether or not to proceed.

"Yes?" Lizzie prompted. "And what did the doctor have to say?"

Fussily, Abby tucked a stray strand of blond hair into her neat coronet. "That I—I'm doing just fine," she repeated. "That is, as well as can be expected—"

"Well, I declare, those are most welcome words! We've all been worryin' over you ever since you weathered that sickly spell right after the school term ended last May. Pa Wheeler must be thrilled to have you at yourself again, Miss Abby." A frown furrowed her brow. "How is it that he happened not to 'company you today?"

Abby seemed flustered by the question and she wrung her hands as she cast about for an answer. "He—he had things to do," she dismissed evasively. "And the heat was too stifling to bring the girls with me. So I slipped away by myself to have a consultation with the good doctor."

"P'rhaps you should have stayed in yourself," Lizzie suggested when she realized that Abigail Wheeler didn't seem quite right and might have grown flighty-minded from the effects of the oppressive heat. "Besides, I'm surprised at Pa for lettin' you venture out all by your lonesome. It's not a'tall like him, since he's usually so protective of you."

"It was my idea. And as I told you, he found some things to occupy himself around the farm," Abby reiterated in a stiff tone that sounded more than a little on edge.

Lizzie gave her a sidelong glance. "You 'n' Pa have words 'bout somethin'?"

"No!" came the curt reply.

Lizzie frowned and stared across the road as she chewed on a splinter of ice. "Hmmm. Well, sometimes a body does 'preciate a bit o' solitary to think 'n' plan, I s'pose."

When Miss Abby only grunted in response, it was plain that her friend was decidedly miffed about something. As if to present yet another clue to her emotional state, the young woman scooted away from Lizzie on the wooden bench and turned toward her, fixing her with a stern expression, much the way she might have taken a wayward pupil to task.

"Don't you worry yourself about me, Lizzie Stone, or go analyzing every move I make! My getting out like I did today is certainly testimony to my renewed strength, isn't it? So I'll not endure so much as one more moment of criticism!"

Stunned, Lizzie stared back. "I truly meant no harm, Miss Abby. Warn't pickin' fault. Just bein' interested, is all. No offense intended."

"None taken!" Miss Abby said but in such a quick, snippish tone that Lizzie knew something was dreadfully wrong.

Silence spiraled between them, prickly and uncomfortable.

"My, it's hot today, isn't it?" Miss Abby spoke as if the unpleasant moment had not just passed between them.

"Hotter'n blue blazes," Lizzie agreed. "I'm glad you decided to stop by so's we could have a glass of lemonade together before you have to hie yourself on home."

"I'm in no hurry. I have all afternoon," Miss Abby said casually. "Alton won't expect me home from the doctor yet, since my visit ended a bit . . . earlier . . . than anticipated. In fact, I passed a bit of time at the general store before I came here. But then I decided to stop by for a visit with you, a woman I could talk to, one who'd understand—" She sniffed in disdain. "—better than *some* folks I know, what I'm going through!"

Lizzie frowned. She took a sip of lemonade as she searched for just the right words to draw Miss Abby out about her puzzling condition yet not goad her into further sharp rejoinders.

"You're still lookin' a wee bit peaked, though you're most assuredly gettin' some color into your cheeks. Just exactly how have you been feelin' of late, Miss Abby?" she invited.

The thin woman seemed to be taking inventory from head to toe. Like a child about to give a public recitation, she situated herself comfortably on the bench and launched into a listing of her symptoms.

"Well, my digestion bothers me a little . . . mornings, in particular. But that will pass for me as it has for other women—"

There was a short pause before the meaning of Abby's words sank in, and Lizzie clapped her hands together in delight. Suddenly the young woman's volatile behavior and cranky disposition made perfect sense.

"Oh, Abby! Do you mean to tell me there's been a miracle after all this time? How wonderful! You 'n' Pa Wheeler must be so excited 'bout the wee one on the way!"

"I'm very happy. Yes. Such joy I've found at last. It really is a miracle—"

Focusing on the expected child, Miss Abby began to chatter with happy plans for the near future. She listed off the many tasks she faced and shared her dreams for the babe, which she hoped would be a fine son.

"Anythin' I can do to help, just call on me," Lizzie said. "It'd be a true labor o' love to turn my sewin' needles to makin' garments for a babe again."

"I'll need so much instruction," Abby admitted. "For all my education, I'm a novice at caring for little ones."

"Don't you worry your head none, Miss Abby. I'm an old hand at birthin' and carin' for babes. I expect Pa will summon the doctor when your time comes, but if you've a need for another woman to talk to, I can be there."

Abby nodded and smiled shyly.

"Alton Wheeler must be fit to bust his buttons, he's so proud!" Lizzie allowed.

"Well . . . yes . . . he's ha—happy," Abby agreed weakly, but her voice lacked passion.

Poor Miss Abby, Lizzie sympathized. She must be wondering how she'd ever manage to nurture a tiny babe to adulthood, keeping the child safe, teaching him or her the ways of the Lord. Still, the woman had already been a stepmother to three young girls, the twins barely past infancy themselves when she'd married their pa, a widower whose beloved wife had died in the process of bringing them into the world. Oh, Miss Abby would be just fine—all she needed was a little encouragement—Lizzie waved aside her own doubts.

"You'll have to be takin' your rest," Lizzie cautioned, noting the pallor beneath the faint tan of Abby's naturally fair skin.

"Oh, I am!" the woman assured her. "And I've been drinking milk, too." She offered up the news with the satisfaction of an obedient child.

"Good." Lizzie nodded approvingly. "And don't forget plenty of fruits and vegetables. And some mod'rate exercise to keep your circ'lation fit."

"Well, Alton says that—," Miss Abby began miserably, her words trailing away.

When it appeared that at the moment Miss Abby was not

willing to reveal her husband's opinion, Lizzie spoke up. "Listen to whatever Pa Wheeler says. He's a wise man with a lot o' common sense. An' bein' as how he's been through it all before, he knows how to advise ya."

"I–I suppose he does."

"So what do the Wheeler girls think—Katie, Molly, and Marissa? They're prob'ly countin' the days, ain't they?"

Abby wrung the hanky in her hands, then set her empty lemonade glass aside and dabbed at the beads of perspiration dotting her brow.

"The girls? Why, we haven't told them yet. Alton's insisting that we keep the birth a secret for a while longer—" Miss Abby's countenance fell. "He's being so mean-spirited about all of this," she wailed. "He keeps cautioning me not to say anything to anyone. But I *had* to tell *someone,* and I felt I could confide in you." She turned an imploring look on Lizzie. "Please! Won't *you* be happy for me?"

"O' course I will! I am!" Lizzie said, then paused thoughtfully. "Sort o' surprises me, though, that Pa Wheeler ain't wantin' to shout the good news from the rooftops. But he must have his reasons, so you'd best humor him. Might be that he's simply afraid his joy will turn to sorrow if he basks in it too soon."

"Yes, I suppose. Things do happen . . . and we've been disappointed so many times before."

Abby fell silent, thinking no doubt of all the times she'd believed herself with child and their hopes had soared only to be shattered.

"Nothin' bad will happen," Lizzie spoke confidently, sensing her friend's fear. "An' there's plenty o' time for makin' announcements. Why, soon there'll be no hidin' the news when you're fairly bloomin' with impendin' motherhood—"

She paused, cocking her head. "Just when *will* we be welcomin' the wee one?"

"I—I'm not quite sure," Miss Abby said, faltering. "Even the doctor doesn't . . . seem . . . to . . ."

The woman's explanations faded away, her expression suddenly so woebegone that it tugged at Lizzie's heart.

"P'rhaps he can tell more when you've advanced a bit," Lizzie suggested. "I've heard tell sometimes even men o' medicine have a hard time predictin' a babe's arrival when the wee one's newly formed in its mama's womb."

In response, Abby simply gave a beleaguered sigh that was as joyless as her recent declarations had been bright with hope.

Lizzie slipped her arm around her friend and gave her a fond pat. "You poor dear. This is all new to you, ain't it, and fearsome, too? One minute you're eager as can be, 'n' the next, wonderin' what on earth you've let yourself in for!"

Abby seemed to draw strength from this evidence of compassionate understanding. "Oh, my heavens, yes! Since I was brought up in the Orphans' Home, I was never around women who were . . . in the family way. I'm afraid I'm painfully ignorant about some things."

Lizzie laughed and smoothed the blond tendrils away from the sweet, perplexed face. "Don't you fret, Miss Abby. You've friends in the neighborhood to look out for you. It'll all come natural, you'll see. After all, you're smarter'n most folks hereabouts. What with our common sense 'n' your book-larnin'—"

At her own utterances, Lizzie's eyes suddenly widened in concern. "Whatever are we goin' to do, Miss Abby?" she gasped. "Our young'uns need you in the schoolroom, but now that you're goin' to be bearin' a babe, 'tain't fittin'—"

"I'm aware of that. And I've informed Alton of that fact . . . persistently."

"You mean . . . he ain't listenin' to you?"

Abby's reply was a curt shake of her head.

Lizzie frowned. "Then Pa Wheeler must confide in some o' the menfolk. They'll have to find a schoolteacher who can fill in for you on short notice. Not only is it not fittin' for a woman in your delicate condition to be teachin' young'uns, but it's not good for *you*, Miss Abby, nor the comin' babe, to be on your feet 'stead of takin' your ease."

Abby seemed to grow flustered once more. "I—I'm sorry I said anything. Maybe Alton's right, and I shouldn't have told you and risked speaking out of turn."

"Now, don't go apologizin'," Lizzie scolded. "The birthin' of a young'un is cause for celebratin'. You'll be a wonderful mama to your new little'un same as you've been to Alton's girls. And I'll be there any time you need me, day or night."

"You're a dear, sweet friend, Lizzie." Abby gave her arm a grateful squeeze.

A few minutes later the younger woman arose abruptly. She fluffed her skirts that had wilted in the heat and humidity, then smoothed the bodice of her dress as she prepared to stroll to the fence where the team waited in the shade.

"I really must be going. I told Alton I wouldn't be late."

"Please take another moment's ease, Miss Abby. It's powerful hot, 'n' it's a ways yet to your place. Let me fetch Doc and Dan a bucket o' water from the cistern to hold 'em 'til they get home."

"That's thoughtful of you, Lizzie. Alton said something about watering them while I was in town. I'm afraid it slipped my mind . . . at least I think it did. My . . . all of a sudden . . . I . . . don't . . . remember."

"No matter," Lizzie said soothingly. "I'll tend to it while you rest up."

"Don't tell Alton I forgot, will you?" Abby whispered.

Lizzie, who had not for a moment considered tattling, gave her a surprised look, but the woman's face appeared so stricken that Lizzie felt obligated to set her mind at ease.

"'Course not. There's no reason to. Heat like we've been havin' of late can addle even the soundest o' minds."

Abby stood in the shade as Lizzie drew two buckets of water, then a third, while the suffering horses almost stomped on her skirts in their haste to quench their thirst.

Then Lizzie accompanied Abby to her wagon and assisted her as she clambered up into the seat.

"Hurry back now," she said. "An' give Pa Wheeler our best."

Lizzie watched as the schoolteacher drove away. Then she reseated herself on the log bench and poured what lemonade remained in the pitcher. Idly she chewed the ice and sipped the sweetly tart beverage as she mused over the strange afternoon.

How odd Miss Abby had seemed. And how puzzling her behavior. Yet, except that today she was thinner and more haggard, she looked like the same Abigail Buckner who had moved into their area several years ago right out of the Orphans' Home. But that was where all resemblance ended. In many ways, Lizzie felt as if she'd been visiting with a stranger.

"Once Miss Abby adjusts," Lizzie decided, collecting the pitcher and glasses and heading for the cabin to begin preparing supper, "she'll be fine. Just fine. Leastways, for Pa Wheeler's sake . . . I sure hope so!"

Lizzie was about to head for the cabin to begin preparing

the evening meal when she glanced out across the pasture and saw her husband, Jeremiah, come loping across the meadow.

Her heart squeezed at the sight of him, his brown hair gleaming golden in the wash of late afternoon sunlight, his complexion burnished to a coppery sheen. Even from here, she could see his lithe build, muscles straining against the faded chambray shirt. He'd filled out some since that awful time when he'd lain still as death for weeks on end. Now, at a glance, folks wouldn't guess that he'd ever been anything but a strong and healthy man.

If only—Lizzie mused. Remembering the wondrous nights of passion they'd shared, the corners of her lips turned up in a wistful smile. She'd belonged to Jeremiah Stone then more than she'd belonged to herself, so perfect was their physical union. It did beat all, though, she thought, that such pairing had never resulted in the babe they'd both wanted. But in the end, she realized, the Lord knew best.

Such precious memories. . . . She studied Jem as he approached. Did he ever yearn, as she did, to rekindle those private moments? Could they know again the passionate oneness they had once known? When he took a notion, Jeremiah was still affectionate. But could there be more than fond pats and kisses?

In that instant, with all the children busy about their chores on other parts of the sprawling farm, she made an impetuous decision. She tidied the tendrils of hair springing about her face and smoothed her skirts, then moved boldly to greet her husband as she had so many times before at the end of his busy workday—

"Hello, darlin'," she murmured as he drew nigh.

Startled at the sound of her voice, he glanced up, his eyes momentarily blank. Then they sparked with recognition.

Lizzie smiled and held out her arms to him, hoping against

hope that he'd hold her tenderly, intimately, as a husband holds a wife he loves dearly and desires.

Almost dutifully, he ducked to slip into Lizzie's outstretched arms. She pressed a warm kiss to his cheek. Then she bravely sought his mouth. But instead of responding, he squirmed beneath her touch and firmly, somewhat impatiently, pulled away.

It was useless to hope . . . futile to dream . . . torment to imagine—

"Run along and play, Jem," Lizzie sighed, releasing him as she often had released the children when they weren't in the mood for affection. "Go swing for a while. It's cool 'neath the tree—"

"Yes, Mama," Jeremiah said in a docile tone. And then, hulk of a man that he appeared to be, he turned back and gave her the quick, contrite hug that revealed what a child he really was. "Bye-bye, Mama."

"Bye-bye, Jeremiah," Lizzie said, smiling through her tears.

Cheerfully he clambered onto the swing that was almost too small for his large frame yet suited his childish mind—all but destroyed by an encounter with that maverick mule.

"You be good and play right here 'til suppertime," Lizzie called after him. "And don't you pester the other boys when they come in from the field. They'll be tired 'n' they need their rest. We've got another big day ahead of us tomorrow 'cause 'fore we know it, school will be startin' again—"

chapter
2

DAYS BLENDED one into another as the dog days of August crept by, sultry and slow. Mornings were damp and dewy; days, breathlessly hot, but evenings hinted of autumn in the air.

As summer paused to step aside for fall, the community stirred itself with preparations for the new school year due to begin in September. And with the days growing shorter, Lizzie, too, crammed each moment full, with little time to think of what used to be.

Mere days from the planned opening of school, Alton halted at Lizzie's farm to see if she needed anything from town. In his pocket was a piece of brown paper listing goods and supplies he would be purchasing for his own family at the general store in Effingham.

"As a matter of fact," Lizzie said, ever grateful for her pa-in-law's thoughtfulness, "we *could* use a few things."

"Draw up the list then, Lizzie-girl, and I'll see to it 'long with my own girls' needs. Anythin' else I can do for you while I'm at it?"

"Well, yes, Pa. Yes there is!" Lizzie felt her pulse gallop as she decided that fitting or not, the moment had come to broach the subject of school with Jeremiah's pa.

"And what might that be?" he asked pleasantly.

"Alton . . . Pa—," Lizzie began reluctantly. "Miss Abby dropped by last month 'n' I understand that congratulations are in order. That is, unless there's been a change since she confided in me last."

He gave her a perplexed stare, cocking his head like a befuddled hound. "What're you drivin' at, Lizzie? Congratulations? For what?"

"For the comin' babe! Nigh on to a month ago she told me about your new little'un, and I can't tell you how happy I am for you both. But at the risk of soundin' indelicate, Pa, the school term's upon us, the young'uns need instructin', 'n' I ain't a'tall sure Miss Abby oughta be the one doin' it—"

Alton stared at Lizzie in horror, his mouth agape. "She . . . Miss Abby . . . told you 'bout . . . a *babe?*"

"That she did," Lizzie said. "She was happy at first, but her happiness was blighted by the way she felt you was takin' the news." She gave him a look of disgust. "Now I can see for myself why the poor thing's plumb sick with worry!"

Alton gave a heavy sigh. "So that's what she told ya," he murmured, shaking his head sadly. "Now that you've been studyin' on it ever since, heaven knows what you must be thinkin' o' me after hearin' Miss Abby's accusations and lamentations."

The silence thundered between them until Lizzie broke it at last. "Pa, I have to say I'm more'n a little disappointed that a good Christian man like you doesn't have enough love to spare for another young'un, but that's none of my affair," she hurried on. "An' if I've gone to meddlin' in what should be 'tween you and Miss Abby, I'm sorry. But this matter of the young'uns' schoolin', now that's somethin' we're all drug into, like it or not. And as the school term is bearin' down upon us, I felt I simply couldn't hold my peace a minute longer."

26

"You're not meddlin', Miss Lizzie. After all, you're fam'ly. If anythin', you've got more of a right to speak up than anyone."

"Well," she said, "I know Miss Abby felt that way when she told me the wonderful news. Women do tend to confide in one 'nother, ya know."

"Just this once I wish Miss Abby'd maintained her silence like I begged her to do," Alton muttered.

"What's done is done, Pa. An' bein' made privy, I've been wonderin' and worryin' ever since."

"Worryin'," Alton snorted softly. "That's all I've been doin'. Worryin'." He lifted eyes shadowed with torment. "What am I goin' to do? What on earth am I goin' to do?"

Lizzie gave a nervous but encouraging laugh. "Why, Pa, you'll do what you've always done. You'll provide for another new babe right along with the others. After all, it's only one more mouth to feed."

It was as if Alton did not hear her. "Jus' tell me, what am I goin' to do with . . . Miss Abby?"

Suddenly Alton Wheeler seemed almost as distant and remote in his own way as Miss Abby had in hers.

Lizzie was fast becoming put out with her father-in-law. "What're you goin' to do? Well, first of all, you'll quit moonin' about the situation. You'll face up to it and do like you done with Mary Katharine and the twins," Lizzie replied matter-of-factly. "You're a good pa. Granted, you ain't as young as you once was, but that don't seem to make much dif'rence with the Lord. You're a heap younger'n Abraham was when Sarah had Isaac!"

Alton's bitter laughter cut short her advice. "But, Lizzie, you don't understand—"

"Ah, but that's where you're purely wrong. I *do* understand. Miss Abby 'n' I, we both know what it's like to want a baby

27

'n' be denied for so dreadful long. After what happened to Jeremiah's mama when she give birth to Marissa and Molly, I can also understand that Miss Abby's cause for joy is your reason for fearful concern. An' I know that you menfolk have to face the burden o' providin' for your family. But the Lord don't make mistakes, Alton Wheeler! So I know, sure as I'm sittin' here, that young'un's meant to be, and you'll be plumb daft over it as soon as it gets here."

"That's just it, Lizzie-girl! O' course I would . . . that is, *if* there was a-goin' to *be* a wee one."

"Wh—what do you mean?"

"Listen to me 'n' listen good. Miss Abby, sh—she *thinks* she's goin' to have a baby. But, I'm tellin' you true—there ain't a-goin' be no little baby. She's just pretendin'. Pretendin' 'til she flat b'lieves it. Pretendin' 'til she's almost got *me* convinced of her bein' in the motherly way."

"Pa! How can this be?"

Alton sighed and it seemed as if the weight of the whole world descended upon him. "Miss Abby's been hankerin' to be a mama so bad that she's got herself b'lievin' it."

"My goodness, I—I hardly know what to say."

"I've been a-tryin' to talk sense into Miss Abby, just like the doc told me to do. But it ain't done a lick o' good. I even sent her back to 'im the other week in hopes *he* could make her face up to the truth. But," he sighed again, "she come home plenty het up with 'im and real put out with me for makin' her go back."

"What a shame," Lizzie murmured, at a loss for words.

"The sad fact is that she ain't a-goin' to back down on her latest notion that we're goin' to have us a babe afore the year's out."

Lizzie had never heard of anything so peculiar in all her born days. "You're sure *you're* not wrong?" she asked. "Miss

Abby has plumped up some here lately. And a woman does
... should ... know these things."

"'Course she's plumped up, Lizzie. She's been eatin' for
two!"

"I declare, Pa, I've never heard tell o' such a thing."

"Neither had I ... not 'til Miss Abby started gettin' these
fanciful ideas. For the past few years, time 'n' again, she'd
inform me we were a-goin' to have a wee one. But things allus
come to naught. An' when Miss Abby fin'ly realized we warn't
ever goin' to have us a babe, she got downright melancholy."

Lizzie nodded in understanding. But she was too stunned
to comment.

"One day last spring when I was out in the wagon," Alton
went on, "I met up with the doc when he was on horseback
makin' rounds through the community. So I asked him 'bout
Miss Abby, 'n' he suggested I bring her to his office. He took
her complete medical hist'ry. She was a sickly child, catchin'
every plague that come 'round in the Orphans' Home. The
good doctor opined that it'd ruined her constitution for
motherhood."

Lizzie could only shake her head. "What crushin' news."

"So much so that Miss Abby's refused to b'lieve it."

"We all have to have our hope to hold on to, Pa."

"But hopin' in this case only aggravates the situation. Doc
took pains to warn me 'bout that. Gen'rally, the womenfolk
who make themselves b'lieve they're in the family way when
they really ain't are folks like Miss Abby who want a babe
more'n anything in the world.

"Doc told me to speak the facts to Miss Abby, not humor
her. But—" Alton hesitated. "—I didn't heed his advice ...
'n' now I'm payin' for my transgression. I jus' couldn't spoil
Miss Abby's sunshiny mood by pointin' out there was no

babe a-comin', that it was jus' somethin' she was livin' out in her head—"

"Poor Miss Abby," Lizzie said sadly. "And you, Pa, must be wild with worry. Ain't there anythin' the doctor can do?"

"There ain't no magic elixir. The doc is 'bout as cornfused as me. This's the first case o' this partic'lar ailment he's handled hisself, 'though he allowed as how he's studied th—this make-b'lieve pregnancy when he was a-larnin' doctorin' up in Chicagy. There's even a high-falutin' name for it. He writ the diagnosis on a slip o' paper iffen we decide to look up a colleague o' his up there."

Alton searched through his worn leather wallet, parting bank notes, then extracted the fragile note penned by the young doctor. "Here it is—the fancy-Dan term for a woman who's got a false notion of impendin' motherhood."

Lizzie accepted the parchment and squinted to make out the blocky lettering: *P–S–E–U–D–O–C–Y–E–S–I–S.*

"Oh, Pa—" Lizzie reached out to touch his arm. "I don't know what to say. I guess I could start by tellin' you how powerful sorry I am, but in fact, I'm not, 'cause Miss Abby's never seemed happier."

"Oh, she's happy, all right. She's so gay that sometimes in her excitement 'bout the comin' child, she almost convinces me the doc is wrong . . . 'cept that, deep down, I know better," he said in a dull voice. "But I don't know what to do 'bout it. Already the other young'uns are startin' to speak of a wee brother or sister, 'n' I haven't the heart to explain 'bout Miss Abby. She seems so normal 'cept for her errant notions."

Lizzie sat for a moment, mulling over the stupefying things she had heard. Then she spoke up. "Pa . . . I hate to bring up another pressin' problem, but what are we goin' to do 'bout schoolin' for all the young'uns?"

Alton sighed deeply. "Miss Abby's wantin' to let folks know

they'll need to locate a new schoolteacher so's she can plan for her confinement. I've waited in hopes she'd come to her senses and serve as the schoolmarm again this term. I'll not allow my Abby to be a laughin'stock," he stated firmly.

"No one will laugh Miss Abby to shame, Pa. We all love her too much for that. 'Stead of makin' fun, they'll be prayin'."

"An' do we need it, 'though I've almost gone 'n' lost my faith over this latest turn o' events," Alton admitted in a dazed whisper. He gave another bitter laugh. "But maybe that's why I'm bein' so sorely tested . . . to skim the dross 'n' impurities from my thinkin' so what remains is pure and strong. That's what's been seein' me through so far, but I'm afeared it's goin' to get worse, much worse, afore it's over."

In all her wildest imaginings, Lizzie couldn't possibly think of anything more disturbing than the news Pa Wheeler had brought. "Why, what do you mean, Pa?"

"It's only the beginnin', Lizzie-girl," Alton said, and his blue eyes filled with tears. "From what I've pieced together, Miss Abby's mama warn't right in the head—the doc called it *dementia*—long afore her death when Abigail was consigned to the Orphans' Home. An' I fear the same for my dear wife."

"Dementia?" Lizzie gasped.

"'Tain't a pleasant prospect for one you love. But Miss Abby's mine, 'n' I'll be true to my word given 'n' p'tect her 'til my dyin' day. An' I'm prayin' that, if I can't watch over her no more, some kind soul will do it for me."

"I'm sure Miss Abby will never want for nothin', Pa," Lizzie murmured.

Alton turned a quizzical eye on her. "Would *you*, be the one, Lizzie?" he asked, his manner urgent. "Would you take keer o' Miss Abby if somethin' happens to me?"

Lizzie didn't hesitate. "O' course, Pa Wheeler, same as

you'd take my place if anythin' happened to me. But enough of this kind o' talk," she said, forcing a heartiness she didn't feel. "Miss Abby's goin' to be fine. Just fine. And so are you. We won't walk this dark valley forever."

"Well, for the here 'n' now, we've got to figger out what to do 'bout the school term—" Alton paused, squinting at her. "Don't reckon you've a hankerin' to be a schoolmarm, have you, Lizzie?"

She gave a startled laugh. "Can't say I have, Pa. I've been blessed with horse sense but not the book-larnin' kind." Her expression brightened. "But I do know a young miss who's pinin' to do that very thing. Fact is, she's pridin' herself on bein' like Miss Abby someday!"

"Is that so? Who's the gal?"

"Brad Mathews's oldest girl, Linda. She'd make a fine schoolmarm ... with your Katie lendin' a hand as her assistant."

Alton whooped when it suddenly appeared as if at least a partial solution was in sight. "By cracky, Lizzie, you're right! Why hadn't I thought o' that myself? You're right as rain, gal. It's like the answer to my prayers."

"That's what I'm thinkin', too—"

"We'd best be askin' her soon."

"No time like the present, Pa. Let me get the young'uns settled, and if you're of a mind, we'll go callin' on Miss Linda Mathews within the hour!"

chapter
3

ALTON GAVE Lizzie a hand up into his wagon, and she settled herself on the spring seat, gripping the edge until her knuckles were white with the effort.

Silence fell between them as Alton reined the massive horses around, and the team plodded from the side yard. Heads bobbing and harness bells jingling, they stepped out onto the trail.

Lizzie wished mightily for words of consolation to offer Jeremiah's pa, but it was as if her mind had grown suddenly numb with the burden of all that she had learned. She devoutly prayed that this would not be the case when they confronted Brad Mathews and his eldest child.

Almost before she was ready, it seemed, the team turned into the short lane leading to the Mathews's cabin. Brad's horse, pastured in the meadow, looked up from his grazing long enough to whinny a greeting to Doc and Dan.

Hearing the approaching wagon as it rumbled through the gate, Brad set aside the double-bit ax he'd been using to chop stove wood and, wiping his hands together, moved forward to greet the afternoon callers.

"Howdy, folks!" he said, smiling warmly when Alton reined in the team as they passed into a shady spot provided by a big cedar tree that Fanny Preston had planted when Lizzie was a child. "What can I do for you today? Somethin' in your grim expressions tells me this ain't no social call."

"You're right," Alton said. "There's trouble . . . 'n' it confronts all o' us. The thing is, we ain't got all the time in the world to be solvin' it, neither."

"I'll do whatever I can to help," Brad assured him. "You can count on me 'n' my girls."

Lizzie felt a surge of relief.

"I'm—we're right glad to hear that, neighbor," Alton said. Nervously he adjusted his fedora and, gazing off across the pasture, cast about for the best way to begin. Then, deciding that there was no path so direct as the unvarnished truth, he launched out, and the words began to tumble from his lips. "Brad, Miss Lizzie 'n' I are here representin' the community. We're needin' to beg a favor of you, 'n' from your girl, Miss Linda."

He paused, shifted his feet, then tried again. "It's like this— Miss Abby's not been well of late. Fact is, she ain't up to teachin' right now. Now, she'd been hopin' to return to the schoolhouse for this upcomin' term, but . . . as her husband who wants to p'tect her . . . well . . . I jus' cain't allow her to go through with it."

"I'm truly grieved to hear it," Brad murmured, then waited, trying to understand what they expected of him.

"Furthermore," Alton finished up, "I've come to the b'lief that what's best for my Miss Abby might be best for the young'uns, too."

"And—?" Brad prompted, as the meaning of Alton's words still failed to reach him.

In that moment Lizzie's thoughts sped back to that day in the blackberry patch when Brad had freed her from the torturous vines that had imprisoned her, only to capture her in his arms and declare his undying love. At the memory, a blush stained her cheeks, then as quickly faded, for she had reminded Brad that, while Jeremiah's mind had been destroyed until he no longer even recalled the sacred vows they had exchanged, she was bound to her husband forever and ever—

Now, mindful of all that could never be between them, Lizzie looked Brad directly in the eye. "We'd like Miss Linda to be our schoolmarm."

Brad gave a startled cry. "Well, what do you know!"

"We wanted to approach you, her father and guardian 'fore we were so bold as to take up the matter with her."

"Oh, my . . . guess I never thought of my little girl as a—a schoolteacher," Brad murmured.

"Well, neighbor, think it over now," Alton suggested. "I know it's a lot to ask. Linda's a big help to you. An' it's a mighty big favor we'd be askin' o' her, too. Teachin' young'uns is no easy task, but we reckoned at this late date, we'd have a dickens of a time findin' a qualified teacher, sight unseen."

"I can understand that." Brad frowned in thought, realizing that with the term almost upon them, the decision must be made soon.

"Besides, we wanted to offer the post to one o' our own first. The wages ain't bad, 'n' most o' the young folks are eager to learn," Lizzie said convincingly.

"An' we know Miss Abby's taught Miss Linda admir'bly," added Alton, "so she'd make a fine tutor, I'll wager."

"She could do it!" Lizzie exclaimed, noting the furrow of concern on her friend's brow. "I know she's young, Brad, but she's a respons'ble girl 'n' sharp as a tack."

"'Twould be a boon to us if she'd consider it," Alton put in when the other man was not quick to reply. "An' she wouldn't have to tackle it all by her lonesome, neither. My Katie could lend a hand. Between the two o' 'em, surely they could fill Miss Abby's place and free 'er of 'er obligation."

"I'm sure sorry to hear . . . that Miss Abby's unwell," Brad said hesitantly, assuming that her general ill health was the reason, even though neither Alton nor Lizzie had sketched in the details. "So you've got my permission to ask Linda 'bout the position, since I can't answer for 'er. But the notion won't be foreign to 'er, since I know that one o' her fondest dreams is to follow in Miss Abby's footsteps someday." For the first time, Brad smiled. "I'll ring the dinner bell. The girls are out in the woods, collectin' herbs 'n' rose hips—"

He crossed to the massive bell that hung suspended between two heavy brace posts, supported by a stout length of iron, and hauled on the bell rope. As the sounds pealed out over the countryside, a lump settled in Lizzie's throat. For that bell that Fanny Preston had clanged so many times to summon her loved ones to the cabin possessed a tone as distinctive as her ma's own voice.

Brad released the cord, then he crooked his head. "Come on into the house. Rosalie made some lemonade before the girls left. We can rest a spell while we wait for 'em."

The three made inconsequential chitchat as they waited for the Mathews girls to appear, with Alton and Lizzie carefully skirting the startling reason behind Miss Abby's inability to serve as the area's schoolteacher. They heard the gay chatter even before they saw the girls coming up the path from the bottomland, their hair flying, their faces flushed from exertion.

The younger girls tumbled into the house, a chorus of cheerful greetings on their lips. As if sensing that she was the focus of the unexpected call, with business so serious that they'd been summoned from their afternoon outing, Linda

Mathews hung back. She halted as her sisters scrambled into the kitchen in search of a refreshing drink, after favoring Alton and Lizzie with polite smiles.

Upon her entrance, Linda had heard her name spoken, had seen all eyes turn to regard her, and self-consciously, she smoothed her hair away from her flushed face. She looked from Alton to Lizzie, then back again, before her eyes sought haven in her pa's unwavering gaze.

Seeing the grim set of Alton's lips and the lines crowding his eyes and observing that Lizzie Stone seemed unusually reflective, the young girl could only wonder what grave problem faced them all. She knew that it took more than simple inconvenience to wipe the smile from Lizzie's lips and the mirth from her eyes.

"Is—is something wrong?"

"Nothin' that can't be fixed." Lizzie set the girl's mind at ease. "We just have a little problem that descended on us quick-like, and we're in dire straits to find a solution."

"If there's anything I can do to help—" The girl smoothed her skirts and eased onto the settee.

"We were hopin' you'd feel that way, Miss Linda, for we have a favor we want to ask of you," Alton said and wrung his felt fedora between his hands.

Linda Mathews offered a tentative smile. "Yes?"

Lizzie drew in a fast breath, realizing the request would be easier for her to pose. "We'd be beholdin' to you, Miss Linda, if you'd do us the honor of servin' in the capacity of schoolmarm for the Salt Creek community."

"What?!" she gasped, her eyes wide. She looked at Alton, Lizzie, then her pa, as if she believed she'd not heard correctly. Or that it had all been some joke. But the solemnity of their expressions convinced her otherwise.

"Please say you will!" Lizzie begged.

"But I—I don't understand—"

"Miss Abby's not well enough to return to the classroom," Brad explained.

"Oh, how dreadful! You're sure?"

"There ain't no mistake, I'm sorry to say," Alton said softly.

"Oh, my goodness—I—I—"

The thoughts swirling through Linda's mind were almost audible. It was clear that she was thrilled by the challenge but almost overwhelmed by the frightening aspects that could spell failure for her and for the young charges placed in her care. She was torn between wanting to accept the position and test her skills, and refusing the job and remaining in the secure niche that had always been hers.

Her eyes swept the little group as if hoping to find her decision mirrored in the eyes of those gathered around.

Alton cleared his throat, staring at a patch of highly polished wood floor. "There's no one amongst our people we'd druther have for the job, Miss Linda. It's yours if you want it and can find it within yourself to accept it on what's not much more'n a moment's notice. Fact is, my girl, Mary Katharine, would be thrilled to help you out and serve as your assistant."

"Between the two o' you, surely you can do it," Lizzie encouraged. "You're both bright, hard-workin' girls, 'n' I can assure you that the young'uns' mamas and papas will be four-square behind you."

"Please say yes, Miss Linda," Alton urged.

"And if you can't say yes right this minute," Lizzie added, "at least don't say no. Promise us you'll think on it, pray over it. We'll be back in a day or two for your answer—"

"But 'tis only fair to know they're needin' to know very soon, daughter," Brad Mathews suggested. "The school term's 'bout to start. So if you know your mind, then make it clear now."

A flustered Linda plucked at the hem of her apron. "This is all so unexpected. I hardly know what to think, what to say—"

"Well, we're hopin' and praying you'll say yes," Lizzie interrupted.

Miss Linda gave a slight nod. "Very well," she breathed. "I'll be honored to serve as the children's teacher. The one thing to blight my complete joy, though, is that it's Miss Abby's ill health that affords me this opportunity."

"Now don't you worry your head none over that," Alton ordered. "I'm seein' to it that Miss Abby's receivin' the best o' care. So you just concentrate on knowin' what a great service you're renderin' to all o' us."

"I only pray I won't be found wanting," said Linda in a small voice.

"'Course you won't," Alton assured in a hearty tone. "But you 'n' my Katie'll have much to do in the next few days. She's free to begin right away, so I hope your fam'ly will be able to spare you, too."

"She has my blessin'," Brad said. "Her sisters 'n' I'll manage."

Lizzie heaved a visible sigh. "I'm so relieved this is settled!"

"Between the two o' you, we'll hope to open the school doors right on schedule," Alton told Linda Mathews.

With the atmosphere decidedly less somber than when Alton and Lizzie arrived at the Mathews' place, the four quickly conspired to set plans in motion for the coming term.

"Praise God! Didn't I tell you everythin' would work out?" Lizzie murmured as she and Alton walked to the wagon.

He shot her an appreciative look. "That you did. I'm 'shamed to say these past months have left me with a faith that's wantin', what with Miss Abby's condition 'n' all. But I'm proud the school will be in good hands," he said as they rumbled down the rutted trail leading to Lizzie's farm. "Now mayhap Miss Abby can get plenty o' rest and concentrate on gettin' well . . . 'cept she don't seem to have any understandin' of just how sickly she is—"

Lizzie reached over and patted his arm, giving it a gentle, encouraging squeeze. She felt a catch of tears as she looked at Alton, seeing him as if with new eyes, and she noticed the sprinkling of gray that now frosted his once coal-black hair. His rugged face bore new lines, etched deeply, that spoke of pain and worry. And his shoulders sagged, where once he'd faced the world, proud and confident.

For the first time Lizzie saw Alton as he really was, and she was startled and saddened to realize that he was no longer the youthful, vigorous man he had once been. Like her own pa before him, Alton was getting old and tired.

"Don't worry, Pa," said Lizzie, trying to offer an encouraging word. "Be like one o' the lilies of the field. They toil not, neither do they spin, yet the good Lord takes care of 'em 'til they outshine King Solomon in all his glory!"

He nodded. "I try to, Miss Lizzie. But sometimes it's powerful hard not to worry. I'm only human. I have my failin's in faith when I look to the future . . . same as anyone else."

"Well, Pa, I'm learnin' that a body can bear whatever comes, if they take it just one day at a time, one moment to the next, with a heart full o' hope for the morrow—"

chapter
4

THE SCHOOL term began amid late summer's stultifying heat.

Autumn arrived with a brief cold snap.

Indian summer then stepped in for a brief visit, bringing warm days and cool nights.

The days grew shorter. Temperatures dipped low. The frost was on the pumpkin, and cornstalks rattled dryly in the fields as the heavy ears hung low, grins of gold behind moustaches of brown matted silks.

"It's gettin' to be fine butcherin' weather," Alton said one evening when he stopped by Lizzie's place. "I spoke with Brad and he allowed as how he'd be free to help me 'n' the boys slaughter your shoats, Lizzie. We'll plan on butcherin' this weekend, maybe, if weather's fittin'. We could slaughter on Sat'day and string the carcasses up in trees so they can hang 'til Monday."

"That'll be fine," Lizzie said. "Cold weather feels like it's finally here to stay. If it ain't rainin' pitchforks 'n' sawlogs, we'll be ready and waitin' come dawn on Saturday."

Friday night found Lizzie's home a hive of activity.

"Lester, sharpen the butcher knives—ever' one, 'n' the cleaver, too. May's well hit the hatchet and poleaxe a lick or two against the stone while you're at it. An' you, Thad! Be a good boy and hustle up a stout pile of kindlin' wood. Fetch up some hickory lengths, too, so's we can build a fire hotter'n blue blazes. It'll take a goodly portion of water to scald three hogs, and we don't want to cause the menfolk to run short o' wood at a crucial point in the process."

"Yes, Ma."

"Maylon!" Lizzie whirled about, calling for her adopted son, born to a man and woman who had died when their cabin north of the Wheeler farm burned in a Thanksgiving Day fire many years before. "You collect the buckets. I'll meet you out back by the cistern, and we'll pump water to fill the castiron butcherin' kettle tonight. That'll make one less task come mornin'. That way I can get up 'fore daylight and get the fire goin'."

"I could do it by myself, Ma."

"No, son, we'll all hafta help one another. Ever' one o' us will be plumb tuckered before the hogs are stowed away to eat at our leisure. Jeremiah," she called to her husband, "you come along with us, so's I can keep an eye on you!"

Lizzie then turned to her only daughter. "An', Harmony, it'll be up to you to get my big pans out o' the pantry. Stack 'em up out o' the way someplace where they'll be handy to take outside when we've a need for 'em on the morrow."

Butchering day began before dawn. Lizzie had scarcely wiped the last breakfast dish and put it back on the shelf when she heard Alton's team pulling into the yard and glanced out to see that he and Brad had already arrived.

The sun arose soon afterward, casting a fiery pink glow over the frosted landscape. The neighbors hailed each other, their words accompanied by wispy clouds of vapor with each breath.

"Mornin', Lizzie!" Alton called. "Me 'n' Brad'll set to work right away. Lemont Gartner's comin' to help, too, so plan on settin' an extry plate at the dinner table. He'll be here directly."

Lizzie gave a happy chuckle. "I'm glad to feed anyone good enough to show up 'n' help!"

"To get some of your good home cookin', bachelor-man Lemont would prob'ly butcher a hog all by his lonesome."

"I'm lookin' forward to sittin' at your table, too," Brad murmured as Lizzie passed by on her way to bring steaming hot coffee to warm them before they started their task. "Wouldn't mind havin' your cookin' on a daily schedule myself."

Their eyes met and spoke volumes. Memories of last summer's episode in the blackberry patch came flooding back with frightening intensity. Until now, however, Lizzie had succeeded in keeping her unsettling feelings for Brad at bay. But his nearness caught her off guard, and she drew in a quick breath.

Shaken, she turned away, wishing, in a helpless little corner of her heart that she could reach out and touch him, let him know she understood. But she dared not.

Alton seemed not to have noticed their brief encounter as he unhitched Doc and Dan and maneuvered them into position so they could help with the pulling.

Then the two men set to work preparing the butchering area. They fed the fire beneath the kettle, placed buckets of fresh water nearby to replenish water lost to slopping when the animals were lowered into the vat, or to cool down the water if the fire burned too hot.

Producing singletrees from the back of Alton's wagon, they hooked up a block and tackle on a heavy limb, then secured the rope, checking to be sure that there was a fast and easy way to tether it to steady the carcass for scraping.

"Lemont's here!" cried one of the children.

"Ready, willin', and able!" Lemont called out as he tossed down the reins of his horse to Lester, who led the animal to the pasture to graze. "Just tell me what you want done 'n' I'll be glad to oblige."

"Let's see how hot the water is," Brad suggested.

"It's hot enough iffen you can get three strokes 'n' no more," Alton reminded him.

Brad zipped his fingers through the steaming water, counting, "One . . . two . . . *youch!*"

Alton laughed. "Pour in a dab o' cistern water to cool it off a dram. Then let's go get Mister Hog!"

Lizzie closed her eyes, trying not to think, not to hear, as Alton, Brad, and Lemont entered the stout pen where the swine were kept and sorted out three fat hogs.

The dull blow was followed by a muffled outcry as an animal fell. Then, there were excited snorts, grunts, and squeals of alarm from the other pigs. In a few moments the deed was done.

Alton and Lemont dragged a hog by a rope attached to its hind hock. Brad came behind, walking carefully, so not to spill the blood that had been gathered in a galvanized bucket.

"Here you go, Miss Lizzie," Alton said, handing her the bucket.

"Harmony!" Lizzie cried. "Run get Mama's whisk! The men're lettin' nothin' go to waste! There'll be 'nough blood sausage for all o' us!"

The men poured buckets of water over the hog, scrubbing at its hide with an old house broom to cleanse it before dipping it in the scalding water so its skin could be scraped free of bristles.

Lizzie settled herself on a stump and idly watched the men work as she began to stir the blood. Steamy heat lifted into the air, and finally when it was cool and running thin, she carried it into the house where she'd be adding corn meal, herbs, seasonings, salt and pepper before forcing it into casings to hang in the smokehouse for preservation.

"Check the water, Brad!" Alton called.

He did, and it was deemed perfect.

"Then let's give this little piggie a bath!" Lemont declared.

"One ... two ... three ... heave!" Alton bawled.

Alton and Lemont, plus a boy or two, hauled on the rope affixed to the block and tackle and swung the hog up, arching it toward the massive black butchering kettle of scalding water. Brad grabbed a hock and guided the beast toward the smoke-blackened, cast-iron vat.

They eased the carcass down into the hot water.

Up it went again, wreathed in a cloud of steaming vapor. Down.

Up. Water dripped from the hide and sizzled as it fell into the licking flames.

Alton tugged at a wiry black bristle. "Perfect! Just perfect!" he decided when the bristle pulled out easily. He tossed it over his shoulder.

The men set to work with scraping spoons, and soon the bristles were mounded in rough piles on the ground, and the black hog exhibited a shiny white hide.

"Refill the kettle, boys! There's more where this'un come from!"

As the men continued their work, Lizzie's tasks increased. She whisked blood until her arm throbbed, and she almost met herself coming and going as she located items that the men required to ease their labors. Soon pans began to stack up on the kitchen table and on the sideboard as she was handed graniteware pans brimming with organs and sweetbreads.

"We won't 'low you to throw out nothin' but the squeal, Lizzie," Lemont remarked.

Lizzie laughed. "Tell me how to fry or boil or bake a squeal, 'n' I'll make use of that, too, 'n' won't *nothin'* go to waste!"

"Prepared by your hand, a squeal might be right tasty," Brad said, winking.

"But probably not very fillin'," Alton concluded.

"Might be noisy goin' down, too," Lemont chimed in.

Although the workday was long and rigorous, there was a festive air about it that everyone, even Jeremiah, enjoyed. And he, too, seemed to relish the company of the neighbors, although their bantering words were lost on him.

"I'd best hie myself on into the house 'n' start dinner," Lizzie said at last, "iffen you don't need me out here. You men are goin' to be famished."

"We're gettin' a traditional hog-butcherin' dinner, ain't we?" asked Alton, looking up from his work.

"Right you are!" Lizzie said. "Fried liver, smothered in onions, fried taters, biscuits, vegetables, plus a pound cake for dessert! An' plenty of tomato catsup for those who want it, or salty vinegar and red pepper sauce for the rest!"

Encouraged by the cheers of approval that went up from the men, Lizzie rushed into the cabin, jerked off her cloak and scarf, hung them on the hook by the door, and slipped on a fresh apron. Then she set about preparing the meal while Harmony took her mother's place out under a tree near the butchering area, standing by to fetch and carry for the men.

An hour later, a harsh scream from the slaughtering area sent a chill up Lizzie's spine. Looking from her kitchen window and seeing them all standing over a body, she didn't take time to throw on a wrap but rushed outside.

Blood was pooling onto Lem's worn, misshapen brogan, and there was a gash in the faded leg of his overalls.

"Wh—what's wrong?"

"Just a little accident, Miss Lizzie," Lemont said, his face pale and waxen. "'Tain't nothin' to speak of."

Lizzie frowned, unconvinced, as she saw the blood bubbling against the worn denim, which was quickly clotted with gore.

"I think we'd better get him to the doctor, Alton," Lizzie said. "You know how Ma felt 'bout barnyard wounds . . . 'n' I feel the self-same way."

"Aw, it's nothin' but a flesh wound, and thanks be to God this once that I've got plenty of flesh!" Lem attempted a laugh, trying to make light of the incident.

"Lem, I dunno—," Alton began. "Maybe you should get a sawbones to take a gander at the cut. 'Tis nasty 'n' deep. An' like Lizzie pointed out . . . 'tis a barnyard wound."

"Aw, I've been hurt worse'n this by far and at times when I was down in the slop, a-wallowin' with my own sows! 'Tis a mere scratch."

"Some scratch," Lizzie complained. "You're bleedin' worse'n a stuck pig."

Still, Lem didn't protest when the men helped him into Lizzie's house and she slapped a clean dishtowel onto his leg to stem the flow. To their horror, the snowy towels were quickly soaked through.

"Lemont, your wound ain't stopped bleedin'," Lizzie said, eyeing the crimson blotches. "An' you've already lost a good bit o' blood."

"Reckon you'll have to stitch me up, Lizzie," he said matter-of-factly. "Or, if you can't, I'll tend to it myself. Get me a sharp needle 'n' a length o' good stout cotton thread, an' I'll do the honors."

"Lemont!" Lizzie gasped, realizing he was serious.

She gave the wound a long look, and although her spirit quailed and her stomach rolled over, she resigned herself to the inevitable task ahead. Moving woodenly, Lizzie collected the necessary materials, taking time to hold the needle in the reservoir of hot water on the range.

"Alton, Brad . . . can't one o' you do somethin' with him?" she begged. "I'd a heap rather he went to the doctor in town. Maybe he could give Lem somethin' for the pain 'n' somethin' to ward off infection—"

"We've tried, an' he's as stubborn as one o' Jeremiah's mules!" fussed Alton. "But he won't be the first feller with homemade stitches."

"If you don't wanta do it, Miss Lizzie, let me know," offered Brad. "I've sewed on buttons a time or two. Might not be neat, but I can guarantee it'll hold!'

"Fools," Lizzie grumbled, "the entire lot o' you!"

"Double the thread a time or two," Lemont instructed in a benign tone, "so's the cotton won't rot away too fast and 'low the wound to split open again afore it's healed."

Lizzie gave him an exasperated look. "All right. But I'm goin' on record one last time as sayin' I wish you'd get proper care. You menfolk just worry me plumb to death with your stubborn ways! Iffen I had such a cut . . . or one o' the young'uns . . . you'd have insisted we see a medical doctor, and you'd have heard no neverminds to the contrary. Now, if there's no changin' your mind, I'm ready. Are you?"

"Ummm . . . well—" Cold sweat popped out on Lemont's high forehead. "'Spose the longer we procrast'nate over the matter, the worse it'll be." He gave a hitching cough, and his callused hands gripped the arms of the chair. "*Sew, woman!*"

"Let's skedaddle on outside, Brad," Alton said hurriedly,

"an' see what's left to be done. We'll leave Miss Lizzie to her task."

She momentarily closed her eyes and breathed a prayer before she jabbed the needle through Lemont's flesh, recoiling when she met resistance before the sharp point slid on through the layers of skin. Gingerly she drew the thread snug but not tight enough to pucker.

After the first wince, the man didn't flinch, and Lizzie was able to forget for a moment that it was flesh she was mending and not fabric.

Once, when she halted to reach for her shears to snip off the thread after forming a knot, Lizzie glanced at the portly farmer and saw that rivers of cold sweat were pouring from his heavily jowled features and that his face was the color of biscuit dough.

"I'm almost done," she whispered, and gave his knee a comforting pat before hurrying as fast as she dared.

"Take your time and do it right, Lizzie. Better you doin' it than me tryin'."

"There y'are," she said, as the shears flashed one last time, and she snipped the thread.

Shaken, Lemont bent forward to roll down the bloody pants leg. "And I thank ye kindly, ma'am."

Lizzie put out her hand. "Wait. Let me look at that leg once more." Studying her neat stitches, she saw that the wound was showing signs of seepage. "I'd feel better if you'd let me apply a vinegar poultice. Mama swore by it. Said it'd discourage putrefaction. An' it'd only take a minute more. I've got lots o' vinegar and plenty o' clean cotton rags—"

With a rough jerk, Lemont slid the pants cuff down around his ankle and onto the brogan that was caked with blood. He got to his feet, gripping the ladderback kitchen chair to steady himself.

"You'd worry and wool me to death with your fussin's and cluckin's, Lizzie Stone! I'll be fine, do you hear? *Fine!* All I need is a hearty meal to pluck up my strength. Ain't nothin' wrong with me now 'ceptin' I'm half-starved!"

Lemont limped to the table and ate a heaping plate of the cooling leftovers.

But Lizzie's appetite was completely gone. And although she and the men urged Lemont to leave early and rest himself in his own bed at home, he refused to depart a moment before the others left for the day. The best she could do was insist that Lem take some leftover liver and fried potatoes to heat up for his evening meal.

Brad, too, accepted slices of the fresh organ meat to take home to his family, as did Alton.

"Until you're better paid for your labors," Lizzie explained. "An' I thank y'all kindly for helpin' out."

"We'll be back come Monday to finish what we started," called Alton as he hitched up the team.

Lizzie and her children waved as their company departed, then they turned toward the house. The children scurried to do their customary chores, but at the end of the day, many tasks remained to claim her attention.

"We had a nice dinner at noon," she said, "so I hope y'all can make do with fresh bread in a bowl with blackberry sauce and milk for supper."

"Everythin' you make tastes good, Ma," Maylon said.

"There'll be better tomorrow," Lizzie promised. "It's the Lord's day, and after we get home from services, I'll put on a spread that'll make you forget we ate skimpy this night."

Long after the children had slipped off to bed, Lizzie was up preparing the blood sausage. She got down the heavy lard press, used the clean gut she'd laboriously cleaned, turned inside out, washed time and again and then soaked in brine, and telescoped it onto the spout. Then she turned the crank, forcing the soft, pliable, ruddy-colored sausage into the casings, which she neatly tied off with a knot every so often.

She heated kettle after kettle of hot water on the wood range and did up dishes, washing pots and pans until her apron was soggy and her clothing was damp, clean down to her skin.

Lizzie was exhausted when she finally let down her hair, bathed quickly, and slipped on a fresh cotton gown. Alone in her snug bedroom, she gave a moment's thought to Jeremiah, who had shared so many nights here with her but was now, child-like, tucked away on his pallet with the boys in the attic. Well, no use to think of what used to be. Besides, she was too tired, she thought with a yawn.

She blew out the lamp, grateful that it was Sunday and that, come morning, the day the Lord had created for rest would offer her a chance to take her ease after church.

As she sank into sleep, Lizzie momentarily jerked awake with a worried thought for Lemont Gartner's welfare. Too exhausted to remain awake long enough to pray that his wound would heal properly and without complications, she dropped off to sleep as a boulder falls into a calm pool. And between one heartbeat and the next, Lizzie Stone was dead to the world.

chapter
5

Lizzie was mentally planning her Sunday dinner when she stepped from the little white church building after the Sunday service. So preoccupied was she, in fact, that she was surprised when the Mathews girls approached the wagon Lester had brought around and invited the Stones for the noon meal.

"We've a fine roast left simmerin' in the oven while we were away," said Jayne. "We'll add potatoes from the root cellar and canned carrots from the pantry. So we can eat almost before you know it."

"Sounds scrumptious," Lizzie sighed. "I must confess we overslept this mornin' 'til I didn't have time to make my usual preparations. We'll be delighted 'n' gratified to join you 'n' your fam'ly."

"You could use some rest from your cooking and other labors, Miss Lizzie," Linda admonished. "When Pa brought home the fresh liver last night, he remarked at how tuckered you were."

Lizzie smiled wanly. "Reckon I'm not as young as I once was."

The day passed quickly and pleasantly, with Katie Wheeler coming to call in the afternoon.

Linda popped corn over the open hearth, and Jayne stirred

fudge on the stove while Brad cracked black walnuts to add when the confection had simmered to the right consistency.

Near the roaring fire, the boys amused themselves with game after game of checkers, and Jeremiah laughed loudly each time someone jumped another player's round token on the red-and-black board.

"It's late, children, we'd best head on home," said Lizzie when the afternoon was far spent. "We've chorin' to do. As long as we've been gone, the fire is like to be plumb out 'n' the cabin drafty. Get your wraps now!"

There were groans all around as the young people wrested themselves from their game. This had been such a pleasant reprieve from the busy cycle of their lives that they were reluctant to leave.

"Thanks, girls, for invitin' us today," Lizzie called when they were ready to depart. "Dinner was one o' the best I can recollect since Mama was livin'!"

"That's because they had the best cook teachin' 'em," Brad pointed out.

"Well, then, I guess I'll just have to exhibit exactly what a cookin' range 'n' I can conspire to do when you 'n' Alton return tomorrow to help my boys work up the shoats now that they've cooled out."

"I'll be lookin' forward to it," Brad said, his eyes shining.

"My young'uns won't be to school in the mornin', Miss Linda," said Lizzie, addressing the young schoolteacher. "But y'all go ahead. I'll cook up enough at noon to send leftovers home with your pa. You gave me respite from cookin' this day, and I plan to return the favor."

On Monday, Maylon, Thad, and Lester stayed home from school to help Alton and Brad cut up the meat and grind the sausage, but they were not allowed to lie abed a moment longer than was customary, since Lizzie summoned them from their slumber at the crack of dawn.

Breakfast was barely over when Alton and Brad arrived, and the boys ran to greet them.

Inside, Lizzie and Harmony rushed through the breakfast dishes, restoring order in the kitchen. But a quarter of an hour had passed before she could throw on her wrap and, burdened beneath the stack of metal pans she carried, join the men.

Already they'd taken one of the carcasses down from the oak limb where it had hung from a singletree, hauled into place by Alton's team.

The men and Lizzie's boys hefted the hog onto a stout table, containing an assortment of saws, axes, and gleaming, sharp knives.

"You want it cut into pork chops or tenderloin?" asked Brad.

"Chops," Lizzie decided. "Jeremiah dearly loves 'em."

"Good enough," Alton said. "You go on back to the kitchen where it's warm, Lizzie, 'n' we'll send the boys in with pans as we fill 'em. With luck, we can start grindin' sausage this afternoon and be a-renderin' down the lard not long after."

By midmorning it seemed that every pan, basin, and kettle Lizzie owned was full of pork cutlets waiting to be fried and stored in stone jars. Huge hams, so big she could hardly wrestle them, needed to be prepared for the smokehouse.

Lizzie put pork chops in the skillet for dinner and soon had potatoes peeled and boiling in a pot of water on the range. While they were cooking to the right consistency for mashing, she lugged in the first ham and set it on the table covered in oilcloth.

Mixing together saltpeter, curing salt, brown sugar, and

black and red pepper, she sprinkled the mixture onto the pale pink meat. Gradually she began to work it into the pork, kneading it until the juices ran. When the meat had absorbed a handful of the salty, seasoned sugar, Lizzie reached into the bowl for another portion and began the process again.

By the time she'd finished the first ham, her shoulders ached and her hands felt as if they were on fire from the coarse salt and stinging peppers. After she'd treated the shoulders and hams from one hog, she instructed Harmony to roll up her sleeves.

"No time like the present for you to learn, honey," Lizzie said, "same as I learned at Granny Preston's side when I was but a tadpole."

An hour later Lizzie cleaned off the table, with the day's salting only partially accomplished. She mopped off the oilcloth with scalding hot water, washing it time and again to cleanse it so that Harmony could set the table.

"What's for dinner, Ma?" Maylon called as the men trooped in, crossed to the basin in the corner, and washed up.

"Pork chops, mashed taters, an ocean o' gravy, corn, candied yams, and apple dumplin's with sweet cream."

"You spoil us, Miss Lizzie," Brad murmured.

"Nonsense! Like the Good Book says, 'The laborer is worthy of his hire,' 'n' feedin' y'all as well as I'm able is the least I can do to show my 'preciation."

"Lemont would be smackin' his lips over this cobbler, Ma," Lester said when the meal ended.

"Lemont!" Lizzie cried with such force that she startled them all. "Has anyone seen Mister Gartner? I meant to go over and see 'bout him yesterday, but I plumb forgot."

"Nope. Not me," Alton said. "I kind of figgered he'd come by today and help out if he warn't busy at his place. Sorta slipped my mind 'bout his injury."

56

"We'll check on him later," Brad promised.

"Later ain't good enough," Lizzie declared. "If you men can spare Lester for a little while, I'd like him to ride over to Lemont's with a plate o' dinner 'n' a big bowl o' dumplin's. My boy can make sure he's all right 'n' report back if he ain't."

"We can spare him for a spell," Alton agreed. "We'll be choppin' scrap meat so's it'll fit through the sausage grinder and cubin' up the lard so's it'll cook down fast onct we start the renderin' process."

"Go then, son," Lizzie said as she packed up foodstuffs for Lemont. "But hurry! The menfolk need you here, 'n' I need a strong boy to start luggin' up Mama's stone jars from the root cellar. I'd a done it myself, but I ain't steppin' foot in that cellar 'til one of you fellers pronounces it free of snakes!"

"Aw, Ma!" Thad laughed. "A snake ain't gonna hurt you."

"Hurt me, maybe not! Scare me so's I think I've already died . . . yes!"

"Reckon the snake'd be more afeared of you than you'd be of it, Lizzie," Alton said. "'Specially if he accidentally got in your way and you threw 'im in the skillet, fried 'im up, and then poured grease over 'im like you'll be a-doin' to the pork chops this afternoon."

Lizzie was struggling to wash the five-gallon stone jars in which she would store the chops when Lester returned. Harmony had just completed salting the last ham, and now they were ready to be put into stout muslin bags to be hung from the rafters in the smokehouse.

"How's Lemont's leg?" she asked.

"He was sittin' by the fire when I arrived. Says his leg's stiff 'n' sore, so he ain't been movin' about much. But his eyes lit up when he seen the vittles. Didn't stay 'til he ate, though. Figgered he could return the pans another time."

Lizzie nodded her approval. "Good. The men need you. Tell 'em I'll be out to help as soon as I can get the chops cooked down. As for Lemont, we'll check on 'im again tonight, Les. An' in the mornin', too. I don't mind sayin' I didn't like the looks of that leg." Under her breath, she muttered, "Men can be so blamed stubborn!"

The afternoon sped by as Lizzie's labors consumed her time and attention. She kept the wood range fired hot, covered its surface with frying pans, and tended the sizzling pork chops as they cooked, salting and peppering them to perfection.

Drawing a jar near the stove, she tested each pork chop to determine if it was done, forked it from the pan, and transferred it to the stone jar. Then she arranged the chops, layer after layer, until they reached almost to the top.

From time to time, Lizzie ladled off the boiling fat that had fried from the meat. When they rendered lard later that afternoon, she would pour the smoking-hot fat on top of the pork chops. Then when the jar was completely filled, more hot lard would be poured to the brim. With a heavy stone lid laid in place on top, a tight seal would form when the fat cooled to a solid.

While Lizzie labored in the kitchen, the men worked as hard outside. All of the meat was finally cut up into the right proportions for Lizzie to fry down. The meat had been chopped and spun through the grinder, the men taking turns cranking the lever until their arms ached with fatigue.

It was like a pleasant respite when they cleaned out the black, cast-iron butchering kettle, then lit a fire under it and poured some water into the huge vat. Slowly they added the cubed fat, rendering it to lard, occasionally ladling out pans full of the sizzling grease as Lizzie needed it to pack the pork chops.

When the men finished with the sausage, it remained for

Lizzie to roll the mounds of ground meat onto the oilcloth-covered table and begin the tedious process of seasoning it with salt, peppers, brown sugar, and sage from her herb garden. Then she would work it through with her fingers, burying her arms to the elbows in meat as she distributed the seasoning throughout.

"Where do you want me to put the cracklin's, Lizzie?" asked Brad.

He was carrying a huge pan of flat, crispy skins left behind after they fed the cooked lard cubes through the iron press to extract the fat that gushed into a bucket held beneath the spout.

"Anywhere you can find to set 'em, Brad. And take a pan for your girls. They're a rare treat when they're fresh and tasty, and even after they get a little stale, they liven up a pan of cornbread."

Brad heaved a long sigh. "I think Al and I will be callin' it a day and goin' home to our fam'lies," he said. "That is, if there's nothin' more we can do for you."

"You won't be goin' without takin' along some fresh meat with our thanks." Lizzie paused long enough to bid the two men good-bye.

Then, seeing that her family was hungry, she hurried into the kitchen and ladled out the vegetable soup from a pot that had been simmering on the stove. Because the table was covered with pans of meat, Lizzie and the children stood in the kitchen or went to the front room to eat, cradling their soup bowls in front of them.

"Anythin' I can do to help, Ma?" Lester asked after he had wiped his mouth and set his bowl in the sink.

Lizzie looked around, thought it over, then ruefully shook her head. "It's sweet of you to offer, son, tired as I know you are. But I'm tellin' you true, you'd only get in my way. And it'd take me longer to tell you than to do it myself."

"All right . . . if you're sure."

"Go on up to bed 'n' rest up for the morrow, Les. You and Maylon will have your work cut out for you, luggin' all o' these stone jars full of meat to the cellar for storage."

Lizzie felt a sense of peace after the children and Jeremiah had gone off to bed, and she worked in the serenity of her kitchen, completing one task before turning to another.

She stuffed the sausage into casings and carried the ropes out into the smokehouse where they'd begin a hickory fire come dawn. For a short while she considered forming the sausage patties and frying them down as she had the pork chops, but as nippy as it was outside, she decided that the work could wait until the next day. Or even the day after that if the cold weather held.

They'd been truly blessed, she realized, as she untied her apron, unbuttoned her greasy housedress and prepared to take a hot bath with what water remained in the kettle on the stove. There was now enough meat to feed the family, along with any guests they might have, until the next butchering season.

By the time Lizzie toweled dry and slid into her roomy gown, her mother's mantel clock was gonging the midnight hour.

She blew out the kitchen lights, then carried her coal oil lamp to the bedroom and brushed her hair a hundred strokes. Then she collapsed against the pillows, feeling almost too weak and tired to throw the coverlets back so she could slide between the sheets.

Exhausted as she was, however, she lay awake, listening to the clock bong once, bong once again, then yet another solitary stroke. One-thirty in the morning, and she hadn't had a wink of sleep!

She'd only begun to drift off when she heard the attic ladder creak, then heard bare feet hit the wood floor.

She sat upright in bed. "Who's there? What's the matter?"

"Mama—?" came a whisper from the darkness. "It's just me—Lester."

"Mmmm? Can't you sleep, son? Me, neither. I can't get Lemont Gartner off my mind. I'm thinkin' the way he refuses to leave my thoughts that maybe we'd best go check on him—"

"I'll hitch up Birdie 'n' Mavis right away, Ma," Lester said, "'cause Lemont Gartner's also the reason I can't sleep!"

chapter
6

LIZZIE'S TEETH were chattering from the cold and nervous apprehension as she threw on her clothing, feeling piqued at the clumsiness of her movements.

Lester was waiting with the mules and wagon when she left the house after throwing another log on the fire to hold it until morning in case they were delayed.

"Seems like it's takin' forever to get there," Lizzie complained as the mules picked their way along the rutted road. A lone cloud had passed over the face of the moon, obscuring its faint glow.

"Won't be long now, Ma," Lester assured her, urging the team on.

"Ain't no sign o' life," she observed as they turned up the short, tree-lined trail leading to Lemont's cabin.

"It's the middle of the night, Ma. Our cabin wouldn't be showin' much life iffen someone chanced to pass by, neither."

"Even so, I'm worried—"

It was true that an aura of evil seemed to hang over the place, and both trespassers felt a clammy finger of fear up their spines.

"Lemont!" Lizzie bawled from her place on the wagon seat,

and goosebumps rippled over her flesh as her cry was flung back in her face. *Lemont*.

"LEMONT!" Once again his name echoed back to her through the wintry night, like singers performing a song in rounds. *LEMONT!*

"I'll go see if I can 'rouse 'im," Lester said. "He's got a stout cabin. He might not be able to hear ya, Ma."

Lester hurried up the walk. "Lemont! Mister Gartner! Are ya in there?"

He rapped loud once. Again. Then a third time.

"Ma, he don't answer."

Lizzie boosted herself from the wagon seat and joined him on the front stoop. "I don't like it, son."

"Me, neither, but—"

Lizzie cleared her throat. "We ain't got no choice, Lester. We're goin' in."

"But what if Mister Gartner's merely sleepin' heavy? That bein' the case, we'll scare the starch out o' him."

"We'll have to take that chance, Lester. Druther that than run the risk of abandonin' the poor man when there ain't another soul around to help 'im."

Lester quietly unlatched the door. Noiselessly they stepped into the dark house. Lizzie shivered. The temperature indoors was only a degree or two warmer than the chill outdoors.

She glanced at the hearth. Not so much as one coal glowed red.

"Mister Gartner?!"

There was no answer.

"He don't seem to be here, Ma."

"Maybe he went someplace."

"Not unless he walked. There's no horses missin'. And Ma—look! There's the plate o' food I brung over. It's settin' right where I laid it. He didn't touch a bite!"

"Then the man's sick as a hound! Lemont's always been a hearty eater."

From an adjoining bedroom issued a low moan—an almost inhuman sound that chilled Lizzie's blood. When the moan became a gurgle, she feared it was a death rattle.

Galvanized into action, she called Lester over. "Quick! Light a lamp, son!"

Instantly he complied and they moved forward, no longer groping in the darkness. Inside the bedroom, they found Lemont sprawled amid a tangle of quilts, shaking and shuddering, his head lolling from side to side.

She lifted aside a corner of the coverlet, eased up Lemont's pant leg, and gave a shrill howl of alarm when she saw the bloated flesh. Angry fingers of red clawed up his pale, hairless leg. Within the wound itself, the cotton thread of Lizzie's neat stitchery had all but disappeared as the leg swelled until each stitch seemed to have created an angry, festering dimple.

"Blood poisonin'! I was afeared this would happen," she said, wringing her hands. "If only I'd pitched a royal fit 'til he'd seen the doctor!"

"It ain't your fault, Ma. You done your best. Mister Gartner can be right contrary when he makes up his mind."

"Yes, but I knew he didn't have a woman to tend 'im. I should've insisted 'til he give in."

"Blame-laying ain't goin' to help none, Mama, and Lemont needs us now more'n ever. Iffen Mister Gartner had been meant to see the doc, then the Lord would've moved his heart to do it. It'll work out—"

"Yes, 'all things work for good for those who love the Lord,'" she quoted, "an' Lemont Gartner does love the Lord. We'll do what we can, Lester, 'n' pray that the good Lord'll do the rest."

Tenderly Lizzie smoothed back the baggy overall as Lester

lifted Lemont's swollen leg. The foul odor of the putrid wound sent them reeling backward. Telltale shoots of fiery red spidered from the site and seemed to climb higher on his leg even as mother and son looked on in horror. Lemont regained consciousness only long enough to scream out in pain before falling into blessed oblivion once again.

"No doubt about it, Lester, it's blood poisonin' . . . just as I feared. And it'll become gangrene soon enough, if it ain't already—"

"W—will Mister Gartner die, Mama?"

"It's for sure he will, Lester, iffen we don't get him to a doctor and get him there fast. I've heard Mama talk of poisonin' of the blood, but I don't recollect what she said to do about it. Maybe there warn't nothin' to be done, 'cept await death."

"We'll get 'im some help, Ma. We'll haul 'im to Effingham. There's a doctor there that I've heard tell is the best in these parts. If we make tracks, we can be there by dawn."

"If he lives that long. We've got to hurry!" Lizzie said. "Fetch some straw 'n' fluff it in the back of the wagon, nice and thick. I'll help Lemont into his coat an' gather quilts."

Mere minutes passed like hours.

"I'll ride back here with Lemont," Lizzie said, smoothing layer after layer of quilts over the sick man after managing to drag him into the waiting wagon. "Don't drive the mules too hard, Lester, but we can't have 'em lallygaggin' either. We've got twelve miles to travel, so pace Birdie and Mavis accordin'ly, 'n' thank the good Lord for the full moon that's breakin' through the clouds to guide us!"

"Giddyap!" Lester's cry echoed through the starry, moon-washed night.

Lizzie's teeth chattered in the bitter cold, but she would not borrow a quilt from the dying man.

A dozen times en route to Effingham, she leaned close, fearing that Lemont had breathed his last. But, each time, when she had almost given him up for dead, he moved or groaned, signaling that the blood was still coursing through his veins.

"We'll soon be there," Lizzie said, as the sun stained the horizon crimson. "Go to the big house—the three-story brick mansion up ahead. An' go around back, son. No doubt one of the servants is up already 'n' will summon the doctor for us."

Almost before they could make their request of the housekeeper who answered their knock, the doctor was at the door. Ushering them into the infirmary, the doctor examined Lemont privately.

"Will he live?" Lizzie blurted when he stepped outside the room where Lemont lay unconscious.

"I don't know," the doctor sighed. "In all of my years of practicing medicine, I've seen many cases of bacteremia— blood poisoning—but I've only witnessed five people who lived. I'm hoping this man will make it six. Does he have any kin?"

"Only a distant cousin in another town. But he has a host o' friends," Lizzie spoke up.

"Then I'll keep him here until he's well enough to discharge from my care."

"We were anticipatin' as much. My son and I have to return to our farm on Salt Creek south and east o' Watson," Lizzie explained. "But I'm sure someone will come back in to Effingham to keep the vigil and set with Mister Gartner."

"You will keep in mind that statistics are not encouraging for those stricken by bacteremia, Missus Stone."

"But with God all things are possible," she mentioned quickly.

"Yes," the doctor admitted, "the Great Physician often takes over where we mere mortals must give up in defeat."

On the way home to Salt Creek, Lizzie was so tuckered out that she fell asleep in the wagon, awakening only once, when Lester pulled into the Mathews' place long enough to share the news with Brad Mathews.

Up and about early, Brad ceased his labors and promised to mount up and ride on to the Wheeler property to bear the unhappy tidings. Then he suggested that perhaps the neighbors could rally around to care for Lemont's chores in his absence and set up a schedule to help tend to his needs in the sickroom in Effingham.

Feeling her burden shift to Brad's strong shoulders, Lizzie proceeded on home with a lighter heart. Yet, numb with exhaustion and worry, she performed her chores by rote. And many times throughout the day, she found herself praying for Lemont Gartner.

At midday, Alton and Brad stopped by her farm. "We're goin' to Effingham to see 'bout Lemont. Don't expect to see us any time soon, unless we're haulin' a coffin—"

"Oh don't say that!" she cried and her face blanched. "That thought's enough to make me pray I don't lay eyes on the pair o' you for a good, long time."

It was five days later when she saw them again.

"How is he?" Lizzie asked, without preamble.

"He's holdin' his own, thank God, although he ain't out o' the woods yet," said Brad. "Still 'n' all, the doc considers it a pure miracle. He says we should come back in three days to see how Lemont's doin' but reckons it'll be a full week 'fore he can leave. Without a wife at home to take care o' him, the infirmary's the best place for him to be."

Lizzie nodded. "An' sleep's the best healer. Lemont needs lots o' rest."

Brad gave her an appraising look. "So do you, Liz. One o' these days, if you don't take better care o' yourself, you're goin' to come down with somethin', too."

"Oh, horsefeathers! Ain't got time for the mis'ries."

But she wasn't so sure as the week wore on, and a sudden rainy spell set in with a cold drizzle that penetrated to the bone. Lizzie sneezed repeatedly during the next few days but shook off the chill and kept on with her tasks, all the while cautioning her young'uns to keep warm, eat hearty, and get plenty of rest.

"*You're* one to talk, young lady!" scolded Alton when the children were out of earshot one day. "You'll be the next'un down if you don't mind!"

Then he went on to explain that he and Brad were on their way to Effingham and would fetch Lem Gartner, who was now deemed well enough to make the journey home to complete his recuperation from his serious illness. "We figgered Jeremiah might like to ride along with us to town. He won't be a speck o' trouble, 'n' you could get yourself a day o' rest, Lizzie-girl." Seeing the unusual pallor in her cheeks, he frowned with concern.

She thought it over for a moment. "That'd be nice for Jem. He admires the both of you so—"

Seeing them off, she took advantage of the rare moment to rest. And almost before her head hit the pillow, she sank away to deep, dreamless sleep. The next thing she knew, night was falling and the wagon was clattering into the side yard, bringing the menfolk back from town.

Lemont looked pale and gaunt, and Lizzie wondered if he should stay with her family for a few days so that she could keep an eye on him, but he flatly refused. When Brad was quick to promise that he'd check on the elderly gent himself, staying with him if need be, Lizzie eyed him suspiciously.

"They're right. You need your rest, Lizzie," Alton spoke up, "now more'n ever. Don't argue, girl."

When she saw the two men exchange a meaningful glance, she felt a stab of fear.

"What's wrong? What're y'all keepin' from me? Tell me. It's worse speculatin' than adjustin' to the truth."

"Well—," Brad began, "we hadn't wanted to make ya fearful . . . but there's a bad sickness goin' around in Effingham."

Alton let out a long sigh. "Yeah, wish we'd brung Lem home three days ago 'stead of waitin' a full week like the doc wanted. Had he knowed the truth hisself, though, the doc would've been the first to send him on home sooner rather than . . . rather than—"

"Rather than what?" Lizzie cried, dreading the answer.

"Rather than expose him 'n' all the rest o' us to . . . smallpox."

"*Smallpox!* Oh, God in heaven, no!"

The men nodded balefully.

"We didn't go into the doctor's house, though, Lizzie," Brad assured her, "an' Lemont left with just the clothes on his back. The 'pox went through when I was but a child, so I'm protected, and Lem says he is, too."

"Pa Wheeler . . . what about you?" Lizzie pivoted to regard him.

He gave a self-conscious shrug and produced a carefree smile. "Heavens to Betsy, girl! You should know by now that I'm too contrary to get took sick. But ain't no use courtin' trouble." He fixed Lizzie with a stern glare. "An' that goes for *all* o' us!"

chapter
7

JEREMIAH WAS the first to complain of feeling ill a week later. Then Maylon. Finally Lester. Even Thad and Harmony seemed listless. When a prickle of red bumps peppered Jeremiah's skin, then swelled to become itchy pustules, Lizzie knew it wasn't just the grippe or influenza. It was variola.

Smallpox!

After Jeremiah's pox appeared, one by one the children broke out with the angry eruptions and became so ill that they appeared lifeless in their beds.

Lizzie was hollow with fright, but she moved from one to the other, bathing feverish brows, spooning broth between trembling lips, adding blanket after blanket when the chills wracked weakened bodies until the very walls vibrated.

When the fever at last overtook her, she was too busy stirring soup over the cookstove to be sure whence the overwhelming heat originated.

Remaining at her post, she mashed vegetables, added meat broth, pressed the ingredients through a sieve, and spooned the thick gruel down the throats of her sick charges until she had little time and no energy or appetite to see to her own bodily needs.

During the course of the illness, the bursting pustules

drained onto the bedding, spreading bacteria, so each day Lizzie boiled the linens and hung them on the line to dry before replacing them on the beds. Then she lugged the most recently soiled linens to the wash vat, where she prayed that strong bleach, harsh lye soap, and boiling hot water would be sufficient to halt the spread of the fearsome disease.

Lizzie willed herself to keep going. She commanded shaky legs to bear her weight about, weary arms to lug in firewood from the big pile outside the door. Then she toted in water even when she grew so faint that she threatened to slosh more out of the vessel and into her shoes than made it to the drinking bucket or to the reservoir on her cookstove.

At the end of the first week, Lizzie staggered into the cabin, shivering with icy sensations one moment and panting with scorching fever the next. She sank into a chair and flung off her wrap but just as quickly retrieved it and hugged it close.

In an adjacent room, a loved one retched miserably. She hauled herself up, grabbed a mop and bucket, and charged ahead to do battle with the dread invader, but all day long her head throbbed, her eyes burned, and her throat constricted in spasms. She tried to take an elixir, but her stomach roiled in protest although it was painfully empty. Realizing she must keep up her strength in order to tend to her loved ones, she forced down a bite or two of food, followed by a draught of patent medicine, then struggled to keep it down.

By nightfall, Lizzie realized that the illness was taking hold. She'd never felt worse in her life!

When she examined her face in the mirror hanging over the washstand, she saw the beginning of a rash spreading over her features. It was only a matter of days, maybe hours, before she, too, would be covered with the noxious pustules. But there would be no one to care for *her* then. Not unless she could nurse the young'uns so they were better by the time the disease drained the last of her meager energy.

"That bein' the case," she whispered, "I'd best take my rest so's I can stave it off as long as possible."

With the cabin strangely quiet and no one thrashing about in fever, no one calling out for water or a change of bedding, she decided to lie down. She'd made the rounds, spooning broth until everyone had been nourished. So now there was a precious moment of respite, although niggling at the back of her mind was the knowledge that she still needed to pump fresh water from the cistern, haul wood to stack right beside the door, and—

"I'll do it later," she promised herself as she stumbled toward her bed. "Besides, if I just lay down a little while, I'll feel better to take care of the young'uns—"

Lizzie sank down on the mattress. The ropes swayed, heightening the wretched sensation of dizziness. But as she pulled her best quilt over her, sleep—restless, delirious sleep—tugged her down into a swirling, chaotic world of darkness.

It was Harmony's cry that eventually dragged Lizzie from her troubled rest. Yet it seemed as if the child were far, far away, in some remote region. For before Lizzie could rouse herself to care for her sick little one, Harmony's crying had ceased, and Lizzie rolled over, gave a shuddering groan, and slipped back into her stupor.

She didn't surface again for long hours, and then, only because winter's cold had penetrated her consciousness. The cabin was like an icebox!

Desperation and duty forced Lizzie to her feet. The four walls of the room reeled around her, and she pitched forward, catching herself against the marble-topped dresser, almost sending her mother's pitcher and ewer crashing off onto the floor. She clutched a chair for support, and on legs that seemed foreign to her body she forced herself toward the parlor and the kitchen beyond, straining for sounds that would signal the state of the rest of her household.

"Oh, my God, don't fail me," Lizzie moaned a prayer. "I must tend to my fam'ly ... please help me not to let 'em down—"

Lizzie shivered until her teeth clattered and her jaws ached with the involuntary effort. She staggered into the kitchen, blinking against the blinding glare that assaulted her eyes.

Then she saw the source of the chill. The back door was open, swaying back and forth on its hinges, admitting the icy breeze as flakes of snow drifted down to settle on the hardwood kitchen floor.

How long has it been that way? Lizzie wondered. Dazed, she realized she must not have latched the door properly when she'd hauled in wood the night before.

Spurred to action, she lurched toward the opening and leaned against the jamb, almost sinking to the floor as she exerted her waning strength to close the door and secure the latch.

Turning, she saw that the fire had died down. No wonder the house was frigid! The door had been hanging open for who knows how long, and in the bargain she'd let the fire go out! It would be hours before the cabin would be cozy again, and just when they all needed the protection of a warm shelter, too.

"Oh, horsefeathers—," she said, choking on a sob of frustration. Try as she would to hold them back, tears spilled from Lizzie's eyes, scorching a trail down her brick-red cheeks. Her head ached something awful!

Not only were the coals on the hearth cold and gray, but the wood range had burned so low she'd have to start all over

74

again with kindling and maybe even coax the blaze along with a slosh of kerosene if the flames didn't catch quickly enough.

"The fire—," Lizzie mumbled, keeping her wandering thoughts on the one essential issue. "Gotta get the fire goin' ... gotta keep my babies warm—"

This time, Lizzie struggled to open the back door. The bracing blast of cold air momentarily revived her, but not being clear-headed enough to throw on a wrap, she walked outside with only her thin dress to shield her from the bitter temperatures. Slipping on the stoop, she barked her shin and would have fallen had her stumbling steps not taken her toward the pump handle, and she held on for dear life.

Orienting herself through a veil of fever, she bent her head in the direction of the woodpile and plunged on. Though she knew her destination was a mere half dozen yards from the doorstep, it might as well have been a mile! How would she ever make it to the pile and back, bringing in a heavy armload of wood?

Tears froze to Lizzie's cheeks. She'd never felt so alone. Her children would surely die, she thought, as helpless as a litter of newborn kittens deprived of their mama's care. There was no one to come to her aid. No one close by to hear her cries. And no one beneath her roof well enough to ride for help. Nor would neighbors welcome the sight of a person covered with the loathsome pox. What could she do?

She thought of Brad Mathews. That day in the blackberry patch, a lifetime ago, when they faced their moment of temptation, he'd promised never to leave her. Come what may, he would stand by her, care for her. And even if they could never know the bliss of love fulfilled, he would be her loyal friend.

She would do the same for him, she knew. If Brad or one of his girls ever needed her, she'd be there quick as a wink.

She breathed his name, not sure whether the words left her lips or merely hummed through her numb brain—

Brad . . . Brad . . . Brad . . . Brad—

Even if he arrived too late to save her, maybe he could still help Jeremiah . . . Lester . . . Maylon . . . Thad . . . Harmony. And if something happened to her, she needed someone to be there in her stead, guiding her young'uns through life, encouraging them to walk in the ways of the Lord, reminding them of the eternal truths that she had shared with them as they gathered each night for Scripture reading and prayer—

She knew what she had to do. Abandoning the woodpile, she veered toward the front yard, moving woodenly across the frozen turf.

In her delirium as she approached, the dinner bell seemed to skitter just out of reach. She gritted her teeth and fixed her sights unwaveringly on the bell, as if by staring it down, she could compel it to stay put. Yet, like a mirage, each time she blinked, the bell seemed farther away than it had just a heartbeat before.

A wind from the northwest howled down from Canada, harsh and rude, and swollen with impending snow, slate-gray clouds scudded across the sky. But Lizzie was oblivious to conditions about her, so intent was she on her goal. Already her entire being was pitched to a frenetic peak.

"There . . . there . . . you're almost there—," she panted encouragement to herself.

Falling against the brace posts, she ran her fingers over them, smooth where the whitewash remained intact, rough and raspy where the paint had been eaten away by sun, wind, and lashing rains. Then she drew herself up, letting the post bear her weight when it appeared that her own frame was unwilling to do so.

The bell cord, which she'd reached with ease so many

times, hovered a hairbreadth beyond her reach, tauntingly, tormentingly. She took a deep breath, strained, then knotted her aching fingers around it.

Lizzie hauled on the rope and tugged. She tugged harder. The bell, so heavy, so solid, stationary even in the buffeting breeze, resisted. Metal grated against cold metal, stiff and unyielding. But Lizzie was determined, too, not so much for herself but for those who were depending on her. At last the stubborn steel jangled to life in her hands.

Clang . . . bong . . . clang . . . bong . . . clang . . . bong.

Sharp and clear the bell tolled, pealing out over the barren countryside, where not a leaf hindered the sound. On a day like this, she hoped, the sound should carry for a country mile. Pray God that Brad, Alton, or even Lemont would hear, would know that Lizzie Stone never rang her dinner bell without a very good reason, and they would come to investigate.

They'd know the bell was hers. For they'd recognize its special tone just as readily as they knew the timbre of her voice.

Lizzie's arm ached from the effort of pulling down on the bell rope. Her fingers were numb from the cold. Her lungs hurt until each breath was such agony that she almost wished it would be her last.

She thought of home—so near and yet so hopelessly far—and pictured herself there with Jem and the children about her, well, strong, and *warm*. But that was merely an elusive dream if she failed to summon help . . . and soon!

Fueled by that desperate thought, Lizzie clutched the rope and pulled hard . . . again . . . and again . . . and again . . . until at last she collapsed to her knees.

Lizzie's head sagged to the side, her fingers loosened on the bell rope, and the incessant pealing slowed to a stop. The clapper bonged listlessly once, twice. Then one last humming gong from the cold steel ball as it struck the bell, faded and melded into the afternoon stillness.

Lizzie had lost all track of time when the solid earth, with its matting of dead grass, beckoned her to lie down and rest, and she fell face down on the ground, cupping her burning cheek in the crook of her elbow. Eventually, Lizzie became one with the cold and knew that death was coming to claim her. She was so tired . . . so very tired. It would be good to see Ma and Pa again, and Harmon, and the others whose love had warmed her over the years—

She wasn't afraid . . . not a bit. The Lord Himself was coming to get her and, instead of going back to the cabin, she'd just go on Home to His place—

The light snow that had begun to fall covered her like a downy blanket. A blue jay swooped down from an evergreen tree and scolded her loudly for the intrusion. But she was unaware of anything but the welcoming cold that somehow left her feeling warm and sleepy as she waited . . . waited—

Soon she could no longer recall exactly why she was waiting . . . and Lizzie Stone lay quiet as death—

chapter
8

CLANG ... BONG ... CLANG ... BONG—
Brad Mathews stepped from his cabin door and stretched. Once outside, he halted and cocked his head, listening. Yes, there it was again. A bell tolling rhythmically. Lizzie Stone's dinner bell! He'd know it anywhere!

But why was she ringing it today? As cold as it had been lately, he knew that her boys would have put in enough firewood, so it shouldn't have been necessary for them to go to the timber to cut an emergency supply. And with the specter of smallpox in the neighborhood, most folks had been staying close to home recently.

Besides, he'd driven by Lizzie's place not too many days ago. He had seen smoke pluming from the chimney and lights winking from the windows. All had seemed well.

Still, a prickle of alarm lifted the hair on the back of his neck. Suddenly he knew. Lizzie wasn't calling her young'uns in to dinner. She was calling for help! For the number of peals that split the early-morning calm far exceeded the measure of earthly years lived out by anyone who might have died an untimely death under her roof.

Brad retraced his steps to the cabin and called his daughters to him. "Girls, I think Miss Lizzie's in dire need. Her bell's

79

tollin' 'n' I'm sure she's tryin' to signal for help. I know the neighbors all agreed we wouldn't go callin' 'til the danger of an epidemic has passed, but I can't rest easy 'til I know Lizzie 'n' her loved ones are all right."

"Oh, Pa!" the girls whispered, eyes wide with fright.

"I'll be all right," he assured them. "I had the pox when I was but a little feller, y'know. But if Lizzie's fam'ly's been infected, it may be a spell afore I see you again. You'll have to carry on in my stead. Think you can do it?"

There was a murmured chorus of agreement. "But what can we do for you, Pa?"

"Just pray, girls. Pray as you've never prayed before—"

Quickly Brad left the house, hastily caught his riding horse and flung himself astride the animal's bare back, gouging its ribs with his heels.

As he galloped down the road, he heard the bell begin to slow between pulls on the rope, and he listened in dismay, not knowing if he should take heart, or fall into despair as the final toll faded with the daylight. Now all that could be heard was the gentle keening of the wind that bandied icy flakes of snow over the frozen landscape.

The mare's hooves drummed over the hard-packed clay. Brad rode her as fast as he dared, fearing she might lose her footing on the slippery ground and take a nasty fall.

When he was within shouting distance of Lizzie's cabin, he bawled her name. "Lizzie! Eliz-a-beth Stone!"

But there was no answer.

He continued to call for her until, spying her still body embracing the cold ground, his cry became a guttural moan of despair. "Oh, my God, no!"

For a crippling moment he believed her to be dead. Then flinging himself from the mare's back, he hit the ground with stunning force but didn't halt to acknowledge the jarring pain. He stumbled toward Lizzie, falling to the ground beside her, battering his knees.

He clutched her to him, gripping her shoulders, hauling her from the ground and into his arms.

"Lizzie, oh, Lizzie." A harsh sob tore from his throat. "My dear, sweet Liz ... don't leave me ... please wake up!"

At the sound, Lizzie's eyes flickered open a slit, and she offered Brad a glazed stare. He whooped with relief and boosted her the rest of the way into his arms. Even with the ugly pox spreading across her flesh, she had never looked more beautiful to him.

"I'm here now," Brad comforted her. "I'll take care o' you, just as you knew I would. Oh, darlin', I don't know how I could've stood havin' you taken from me!"

Brad struggled to the house beneath Lizzie's dead weight. He looked around. The deathly stillness frightened him, and he tried not to consider what he might find after he'd tended Lizzie and dared search the cabin.

Quickly Brad tucked Lizzie into bed and drew the covers up around her ears. Then he lost no time in moving through the house, taking inventory of the other dazed and delirious victims of the illness.

All the children and Jeremiah, too, had been stricken, but it was Maylon and Jem who seemed to be faring worst of all, and Brad feared for their lives.

He knew no respite as he moved from one end of the cabin to the other, dealing with each new crisis as it arose, a new chore presenting itself almost before the last had been completed.

Disturbed by the commotion, Harmony, Lester, and Thad awakened. Brad tenderly spooned warm broth into their mouths, pouring cups of cold water and urging them to drink a sip. When they asked for Lizzie, he reassured them about their mama, promising to care for them in her place.

Helping Lester out of his soiled nightshirt, Brad produced a clean one from the chifforobe, then inquired as to where the linens were stored so he could change the youth's pallet. He bathed Harmony's swollen, pock-marked face with a luke-warm cloth, then settled her more comfortably in her bed.

Maylon and Jeremiah were too ill to question, so Brad trickled broth into their mouths, then stroked their throats to encourage them to swallow. The best he could do was force a little broth and a sip of water into them before he was resigned to temporary defeat, vowing he would try again later.

In the meantime he bathed them, drew off their night-clothes and exchanged them for fresh ones, then laboriously changed the sheeting on their beds and washed the soiled ones. His back was aching by the time he had hung the last dripping sheet on Lizzie's clothesline and turned back to the house.

Darkness had long since fallen when Brad paused to take stock of the situation. With several of the family critically ill, he could not abandon them for the night. Still, he knew that he owed his daughters further explanation.

He set out for his farm, tethered his horse, then approached the cabin but did not go in. Hailing the three girls, he waited a long moment until they appeared, framed in the open doorway.

"It's me . . . your pa! There's bad sickness at Lizzie's place. It's the pox!" Then when they made a move forward as if to fetch him into the house, he yelled, "Stay back! Don't come near me!"

"Pa!" Their cry was a mournful wail.

"I told you I'll be all right. I'm immune, but you girls ain't.

This is a serious sickness, so you must listen careful. I'll be stayin' with Lizzie's family to tend the sick. You girls keep things goin' at home as best you can. Don't go anywhere . . . and don't let any callers venture into the cabin. It ain't safe!"

Brad calmly gave instructions for the girls to bundle up extra bed linens and a change or two of clothing.

"Pack the goods in a poke, 'n' I'll pick it up on my way back to Lizzie's. I'm goin' to ride over to the teacherage 'n' see 'bout your sister and Miss Katie. Then I'll post a notice on the door that there won't be no classes 'til this plague passes. I must tell Linda and Miss Mary Katharine to keep their distance!"

"Miss Katie got sick the last day we had classes, Pa," said Jayne, "but it was before you brought Mister Gartner home from Effingham. So maybe she's ill with somethin' else."

"Weak as she is, if Alton bore the germ home, like as not she's caught the pox," muttered Brad, reeling from the news.

He dug in his heels, urging his horse into a brisk canter, his heart in his throat. What if it were already too late to warn Linda? What if he found her lying on her bed, just as he had found the Stone family? But her friend Katie wasn't with her! Linda was alone! He redoubled his speed.

When Brad drew near the teacher's house, he hailed the cabin and was rewarded almost immediately as the door was flung open and Linda ran out onto the hard-packed ground.

"Ho, Linda! Don't come near!" Brad warned. "I may be carryin' the pox! Are you well?"

"I'm well, Pa," Linda called back, "but Katie was very sick. I guess she exposed me and all of the students to what was ailing her before she went home. But I really don't think it was the pox. If so, there's nothing we can do now . . . nothing except pray."

"An' dig graves," he muttered under his breath.

"Oh, Pa!" gasped Linda. "Is it that bad?"

He nodded. "'Twill be a pure miracle if Jeremiah and Maylon are among the livin' come mornin'. Dear as those boys are to me, and sick as their ma is, they deserve a friend with 'em when they breathe their last."

He instructed Linda to letter a sign for the door of the schoolhouse, suspending classes until further notice, cautioned her not to open her door to a soul, then reined his horse around and headed back along the trail.

When Brad arrived at his farmstead, he found a poke sack filled and waiting for him. Hoisting it up behind him, he rode on to Lizzie's house at a dead run, passing Lemont Gartner's place with hardly more than a passing thought for the welfare of the aging farmer. He'd have to get around to Lemont's place when things settled down at the Stones'.

The fire had died down by the time Brad returned to Lizzie's cabin. He threw a log on the fire, then hurried into her bedroom. Finding her sleeping quietly, he clambered up into the attic and peered at Jeremiah and Maylon. His heart sank. From the looks of him, Maylon wasn't long for this world.

Almost before Brad knew it, the lad had passed away, quietly, without a sound. One instant, he was breathing. The next, he had departed this life.

Jem's breathing was labored, as if at any moment death would snatch him, too, from among the living. He couldn't die! What would become of Lizzie if she lost son and husband in the same day? Awkwardly Brad hefted Jeremiah onto his shoulder and proceeded down the rickety attic ladder.

Laying down his burden, Brad fixed a pallet by the hearth, then covered Jem warmly.

Throughout the long night, forcing his eyes open to keep the vigil, Brad never left the younger man's side. Just before dawn, Jeremiah struggled, attempting to rise. His throat convulsed. His lips worked, but no words came forth.

Jem stared at Brad with burning eyes. In that moment a rare communication passed between them. And within minutes, Jeremiah Stone was dead.

Brad cradled Jeremiah's body to him and sobbed out the grief that would be Lizzie's when she learned of her husband's passing.

"Now you will know, Jeremiah . . . even as you are known," whispered Brad and tenderly closed Jem's eyes.

Shoulders sagging, Brad picked up the lantern, shrugged into his coat, and strode to the shed to retrieve a grubbing hoe and spade.

Dawn was breaking in fiery shafts of crimson light when he finally finished opening the graves beside the plot where Harmon Childers lay. Unable to contain the tears, Brad wept as he lugged two coffins from the loft, struggling to get the boxes Jeremiah himself had built into the house that he might prepare the two bodies for a proper burial.

Brad tried not to think beyond the moment, for if more in the household died, he might have to consign them to interment wrapped in quilts.

"Halloo! Ho, Brad!"

Brad was attempting to back the wagon up to the door, wondering how he'd wrest the loaded coffins from their resting place in the cabin, when he heard his name floating to him on the crisp early morning air.

Startled, for in some ways he felt like the only person alive on earth, Brad looked up, staring as if he'd seen an apparition. It was Lemont Gartner.

"Is there trouble, neighbor?" inquired Lemont. "I've been stickin' close to my own hearth, so I ain't heared any neighborhood news."

Brad halted. "The worst kind, Lem. Death. Maylon . . . 'n' Jeremiah—" He turned away, wiping his face on his sleeve. "I feel like I've lost loved ones of my own, so dear to me they were."

Lemont's lower lip quivered. He was silent as he dismounted and tethered his horse to a fencepost near the gate.

"I'll lend a hand, friend," he volunteered, his voice cracking with emotion. "'Tis the least I can do since them two . . . was like fam'ly to me, too."

The men panted for breath as they slid the second coffin up onto the wagon bed and seesawed it into place for the ride to the graveyard.

Lemont stepped back into the cabin. He crossed to the mantel, plucked down Lizzie's Bible, then limped toward the door, and handed it to Brad. "I ain't much of a one for words. But I'm hopin' you'll find a few to say over the remains."

Brad swallowed hard. "We'd best set about our sorry business, for the livin' have dire need of our presence afore they, too, go the way of the departed—"

He clucked to Jeremiah's faithful old mules, and the wagon wheels creaked slowly over the packed ground. When they arrived at the burial plot, the two men lowered the coffins into the waiting graves that Brad had hastily dug.

Lemont gulped a sob.

Brad's face was ashen. For a moment he swayed as if about to collapse beneath the weight of grief and the burden of responsibility awaiting him back at the cabin.

Clutching Lizzie's Bible to his breast, he lifted his tear-dampened face toward the heavens. At that moment a shaft of sunlight pierced the dark clouds and illuminated the very patch of ground that had been opened to receive and embrace two dear members of the community.

"I will lift up mine eyes unto the hills—," Brad began. His

voice took on strength as he read on, drawing power from the Word of God and finding comfort in its enduring promises.

"Amen," finished Brad.

"Amen," echoed Lemont Gartner and drew his sleeve across his eyes.

Then they silently reached for the spades and began shoveling a blanket of earth over the stark boxes.

"What are we goin' to do now?" Lemont asked when they'd finished their grim task and tossed their shovels into the back of the wagon.

Birdie glanced toward the mounded earth as if realizing that it was her master's final resting place and that never again would she hear his voice in the pasture or feel his fond caress.

"I don't know," Brad replied. "I'm almost too weary to think. But the news must be passed to those as have a right to know. Jem was Alton's son."

"That he was. An' the news will break his old heart. Iffen you don't mind, Bradley, I'll stay with Miss Lizzie 'n' her fam'ly. You know Alton better'n I do, so I'm thinkin' he druther hear the bad tidin's from you."

Brad shook his head, trying to clear it. Maybe if he got a few minutes' sleep, he'd be better able to think how to break the news. But there would not be an easy way to tell a man he'd lost the only son he would ever have.

chapter
9

THE SUN was lifting high in the sky when Brad reined his horse onto the narrow lane that led to Alton and Miss Abigail's farm. Even before he reached the cabin, he sensed that the general inactivity about the place was ominous.

"Halloo!" Brad bellowed. His echo bounced off the timber and was flung back at him. "Anyone home?"

A chicken squawked in the coop. A pig grunted behind the farrowing pen. There was no other response.

Brad slid from his horse. His numb feet tingled as they hit the ground. With a growing sense of unease, he made his way to the cabin and knocked on the door. When there was no answer, he beat upon it again. Then he glanced up to see a plume of smoke drifting from the chimney.

He was about to test the latch and walk in, when Katie opened the door a crack. Her face was red and mottled, her hair a disheveled tangle.

"Miss Katie, you're bad sick—"

"I've had the pox. I've never felt so awful . . . thought I was going to die—" A spasm passed through her, and tears of fresh misery welled in her eyes.

"Your mama and pa? An' the twins? Were they took sick?"

The girl shook her head, disoriented, and gave him a

confused stare. "I—I don't know. I just got up to get a drink of water from the bucket, and I heard you at the door . . . so I answered. I—I don't exactly know where the others are."

Brad stepped inside. The room was warm. Someone had been well enough to tend the fire.

"Go back to bed, Miss Katie. You're too weak to be up."

She seemed to float as if she were moving in another realm, and soon she disappeared into the small room Alton had constructed as an addition to the original structure.

Stealthily Brad moved through the quiet cabin, calling for the twins, for Miss Abby, for Alton. There was no answer. He called again.

At last he heard a sleepy voice, then Molly's round freckled face appeared in the attic opening.

She stared down at him in surprise. "Mister Mathews! Wh—what are you doing here? Is something wrong?"

"Maybe you can tell me. Are you sick?"

She hesitated as if conducting a quick evaluation. "I don't think so. Just tired. What time is it?"

Brad consulted his pocket watch. "Half past ten in the mornin'."

"Uh . . . I guess Marissa and I overslept. Katie's been so sick, though she's better now . . . an' we've been nursing her, and . . . well, I guess Mama just didn't call us."

"What about Miss Abby 'n' your pa?"

"They're fine. Miss Abby's been a help with Katie. She . . . Mama . . . has been a bit confused. But otherwise, she seems all right."

"And your pa? Molly, I ain't seen him. The horses are in the pasture, but he don't answer."

"Pa? He was helpin' us with Mary Katharine yesterday, but he said he needed to rest and took to his bed early in the afternoon. He didn't arise for supper. But I allowed as how he needed his sleep more. We're all dreadfully tired—"

"Where's Miss Abby?" Brad broke in.

"I don't know," Molly repeated. "If you'll wait, Mister Mathews, I'll get dressed and join you. Surely she's here somewhere. Mama told Marissa and me she'd see to Katie if she needed anything during the night."

Molly disappeared, and thumps issued from overhead. Molly's twin, Marissa, apparently out of sorts, was not happy to be disturbed.

"Now get up!" Molly said with gentle firmness. "We're needed downstairs. The day's half gone while we've been lying abed."

Hastily Molly threw on her clothing, and Brad watched as she placed her foot on the top rung and descended the attic ladder.

"I think we'd better check your ma 'n' pa's room, Molly."

Together, they stood outside the door. "Miss Abby?" Brad called. "Miss Abby!"

There was no answer.

Molly gave Brad a fearful look, then steeled herself and grimly approached the closed door. Knocking, she spoke up. "Pa? Mama?"

Brad rapped harder. "Al? You in there? Miss Abby?"

As Brad was inwardly debating the propriety of entering the room, uninvited, Miss Abby twisted the knob and opened the door. Knitting in hand, her eyes seemed vacant and lusterless as she peered out, wondering about the disturbance.

"Well, Mister Mathews," she trilled, suddenly animated. "How nice of you to come calling. Did Lizzie stop in to visit with me while I'm in my confinement? I'll put on water for tea—"

"I'm afraid I'm not here for a social call, Miss Abby," Brad

91

spoke in a tired voice. "I've come to check on your fam'ly. And to speak with Alton. Is he able to be up 'n' about?"

Miss Abby patted her blond hair into place. "He's fine," she maintained happily, "just fine. But our Katie is certainly suffering a sickly spell."

"Can I speak with Alton?"

Miss Abby placed her finger to her lips. "Shhhh! Not now! He's asleep. Maybe if we take tea, he'll awaken before you leave."

"Asleep?"

"Sleeping like a baby. As peacefully as our dear little one when he . . . or she . . . gets here—"

Brad's eyes were drawn to Miss Abby's slim figure. He hadn't been told. But, then, maybe she wasn't far enough along. Looking to Molly for explanation, he read the truth in her level gaze. A coming babe was all in Miss Abby's poor tormented mind. No wonder Alton hadn't thought her up to schooling the young'uns!

"Miss Abby, you—you're *sure* Alton is asleep?"

She thrust out her chin. "Of course I am. Really, Mister Mathews, I'm not simpleminded." Her voice chilled a degree. "He's sleeping like an innocent child without a care in the world."

"Miss Abby, it's terribly important that I see him. Would you wake him?"

"I'm afraid he needs his rest," she said sternly. Then she relented. "But . . . if, as you say, it's imperative . . . very well." With a bright smile, she excused herself and stepped into the bedroom.

Brad and Molly made no move to follow. They exchanged quick, perturbed glances, reluctant to speak their thoughts. Instead, when they heard Miss Abby's soft voice coming from within the room, they leaned forward, eager to hear Alton's response.

"Alton . . . darling . . . Brad Mathews is here to see you. Time to get up, dear. He says he has something very important to tell you and that it simply can't wait. Poor man . . . you're so tired . . . so very tired, aren't you? You must get your rest then. Our baby needs a strong pa—"

The floorboards creaked, and Miss Abby reappeared.

"Dear Lord, is he—?!" Brad began.

"I'm sorry." Miss Abby was firm as she closed the door solidly behind her. "Alton really mustn't be disturbed just now. Perhaps later—"

"No, Miss Abby!" Brad's protest was more vigorous than he had intended.

Frightened, she recoiled, and a look of horror and dread splashed into her eyes before it was instantly quelled, hidden behind the blank gaze. Her lips worked, but no sound came forth.

"You *can't* wake him up, can you? Can you?"

She glared up at him, piqued. "Of course I can."

Molly took a step forward, intent on entering the small bedroom, but Brad clutched her arm, restraining her.

"No. Let me, Molly. Please. It's for the best if I go in first."

Compelled to learn the truth, Brad brushed past Miss Abby and entered the dim room where the curtains were drawn tightly across the windows.

"Alton . . . it's me . . . Brad. Wake up, Alton!"

He touched the mound beneath the quilt, intent on shaking his friend awake, but when his hand came to rest on the stony, unyielding form, he realized that the worst of his fears was true.

He drew back the coverlet. There, to his horror, was mute evidence of the ravages of the disease—the purplish blotches left by the pox. *Alton Wheeler was dead!* The knowledge hit Brad like a hammer blow.

Dazed, he made his way from the room.

Looking up from her chair near the hearth, where she was sewing on a tiny baby blanket, Miss Abby gave him a contented smile.

"See? Sleeping like an infant, isn't he?" she said, her mood changing to one of smug satisfaction.

It was too much for Brad. Something snapped deep within him. "You crazy woman! Alton's not asleep . . . the man's dead. Do you hear me? *Dead!*"

Miss Abby's mouth dropped open. She stared at Brad, utterly aghast.

"How dare you say such things?!" Abby cried as her small form quivered with indignation. "I just talked to him. He most certainly is not dead!"

"He is!"

The twins looked from Brad to their stepmother, then back again. "Pa's . . . dead?" whimpered Molly.

"No . . . oh, *no!* Not Pa!" wailed Marissa. "Oh, please, no, not Pa . . . not Pa—"

"Tell me it's not true!" Molly begged. "Please say it's not true."

"Molly . . . Marissa—" A creaking floorboard drew Brad's attention to Mary Katharine's presence as she crept into the room. "—Miss Katie. I can't tell you how sorry I am that your pa's gone. I wish I could tell you it's all a mistake and that he'll be wakin' up soon. But I can't. I won't deny the truth as your mama's been doing. I'm sorry . . . so sorry—"

The girls began to cry. Molly fetched handkerchiefs and pressed them into her sisters' hands. But Abby stood dry-eyed, confused by the circumstances around her. Then she clasped the baby garment to her, her fingers working frantically.

"Wh—what are we going to do?" Molly asked.

"What I have already done this very mornin' for Jeremiah and Maylon," Brad said softly, "conduct a Christian burial. I'll consider it an honor to inter a man as fine and respected as your pa. He was my friend, too, y'know. Is there a burial box in the loft?"

"Two," Molly said. "There was the one Pa always kept on hand. And not long ago, he made another . . . just in case there was a need." Her eyes filled with fresh tears.

"I'll open a grave beside Sue Ellen's, 'n' tend to the burial."

Abby, who had been gazing unseeingly, was spurred to speech again. "Burial? For whom? My dear Mister Mathews, what *are* you talking about?" she asked in an arch manner. "Your behavior is despicable. I'm afraid I'm going to have to ask you to leave."

"Mister Mathews, please stay," Molly said. "Pay Miss Abby no mind. She doesn't know what she's sayin' these days."

But Brad would not give up. He felt he must make the former schoolmarm understand. Surely a woman of her former intelligence could comprehend her husband's passing, if presented the facts clearly and carefully.

"Miss Abby, Alton . . . is . . . gone. He's gone to his final reward, like the Good Book says. We'll bury him shortly 'n' let the good earth claim the shell he's cast off."

Once more Abby's mouth dropped open. "Why, the nerve! I won't let you do that! And us convinced you were Alton's friend . . . and ours! You're daft, completely daft!" Outraged, she whirled to face the girls. "When Alton awakens, I fear he'll throw this man out by the scruff of his neck for coming here and upsetting a woman who's in the family condition . . . about to give birth any day—"

"Oh, God, have mercy—," Brad whispered. "Girls, we've got to do something. Molly and Marissa, can you take Miss Abby for a walk? I can't deal with her and face the unhappy task at hand, too."

"We'll take care of her," promised Molly, putting her arm around the distraught woman.

"And you, Mary Katharine, hie yourself on back to your bed so's you can gain back your strength." When the young woman hesitated in the doorway, Brad glanced at her before entering the room where Alton lay. "How long's your stepmama been this way?"

"Oh, for months," she sighed softly. "And she's getting worse all the time ... more confused ... as you've just seen for yourself."

"I had no idea."

"She's suffering from something Pa called de—men—tia, but we just can't consign her to that horrible institution for such people. Still, with Pa ... gone ... I don't know what on earth we'll do with Miss Abby."

"You'll do the best you can," Brad said simply. "The Lord will provide. An' surely those who survive this terrible plague will do what they can to ease your plight. Now, I'd best tend to your pa, Miss Katie. Go on now. Take your rest. The twins ... 'n' Miss Abby, too ... need you somethin' dreadful."

While Katie crept to her quarters, Brad fetched a coffin, grunting as he hefted it to a wooden sled. Then he hitched up his horse and returned to the house for the body of his dear friend.

Trying not to think, he boosted the big man's body onto his shoulders and struggled through the cabin and out to the sled. Long minutes passed before he was able to hammer the lid into place and depart for the burial plot.

Brad had lowered the box into the gaping grave when a soft

sniffle alerted him to the fact that he was not alone. He glanced up to see the twins approaching.

"We came to be present at Pa's buryin'," Marissa explained.

They bowed in sorrow as Brad spoke words from the Good Book, words that brought some measure of comfort to their grieving hearts. Then, laying the body of their beloved father to rest beside their mother, Alton's twin daughters echoed Brad's litany of faith and hope:

"Amen—"

So be it.

chapter
10

FOR DAYS Lizzie, weakened by illness and delirious with fever, thrashed about on her feather tick, too sick to be told of her great loss. While Brad tended to her, throwing all his resources in the fight for her life, he prayed for wisdom to cushion the news so she would be able to bear it when the time came.

One by one, Lester, Thad, and Harmony were well enough to be up for short periods of time before retiring once again to their sickbeds to continue their recuperation.

As they were told about the dear ones who had succumbed to the grievous plague, Harmony wept, and the boys retreated into stoic silence. But Brad suspected that the chilling truth had penetrated their senses even as they, too, lay locked in the very jaws of death.

"Don't say nothin'," said Lemont when his young charges came to the table to eat the soup he'd prepared, allowing Brad an afternoon with his daughters. "Your mama don't know yet 'bout your brother Maylon and your pa, 'n' we don't want her to hear 'til she's a heap stronger. Such a shock could set her back."

There were solemn nods and murmured words of agreement.

"Your poor ma's done gone through a passel o' trouble—'nuff to try the patience o' Job hisself," said Lemont. "I'm just hopin' her faith won't give way under this latest trial . . . like your Uncle Rory done."

"Never!" Lester said stoutly. "Never—" But the boy's declaration seemed designed more to convince himself than to reassure their neighbor.

He knew, right along with the others, that in losing her first husband, Harmon, followed by her ma and pa and now her adopted son, Maylon, and her beloved husband, Jeremiah, Lizzie had withstood about as much grief as a body could be expected to bear in one lifetime!

Now it was Brad, in Lizzie's stead, who gathered the family at day's end for encouraging words from the Scriptures and a few words of prayer.

"Lord, grant me the wisdom to know how to tell Miss Lizzie the hard news about her loved ones, and give her the grace to hear me out—"

"Amen—," her children quietly whispered.

Lester, Thad, and Harmony, with the resilience of the young, gradually began to bloom again with good health. With their appetites revived, Brad spent most of his time in the kitchen, stirring up rich stews, frying rabbits he'd caught in snares or managed to down with his rifle when they bounded from windrows in the pasture. To further tempt their palates, his daughters created appetizing confections in the Mathews' cabin to restore the pounds lost to the ravages of illness.

Lizzie was slower to rebound, even after it was finally certain that she would not be the next victim of the disease that had raged through the Salt Creek community for at least a month.

In fact, it was a full three weeks before she blinked her eyes open and focused on Brad. For the first time since he'd found her unconscious with the bell rope still clutched in her fingers, she looked up at him with startled recognition.

"Wh—what . . . are *you* . . . doin' here?" Her fingers flew to her throat and she blinked rapidly, a look of dazed uncertainty clouding her eyes as she tried to remember.

"You've been sick, Lizzie," Brad explained, drawing up a chair near her sickbed. "Real sick. We thought you weren't a-goin' to make it there for a while."

"Oh, my . . . I do feel . . . plumb wore out . . . 'n' weak—"

"An' it's no wonder you're weak, gal! You've taken precious little nourishment these past days. But," he added, brightening, "at least you're outa danger now."

Lizzie looked toward the curtained window, squinting against the glare of a sunny, snow-draped winter day, almost blinding in its intensity.

"Wh—what day is it?"

Brad supplied the date.

"Land o' Goshen!" Lizzie tried to sit up, found she could not, and fell back against the pillows. "That's . . . a month later'n . . . I remember it bein'. You're funnin' me . . . ain't ya, Brad?"

"I told you, Lizzie-girl, you've been outa your head with fever. The young'uns, too. Y'all have been too sick to remember much—"

"Oh, dear God, my children!" Lizzie cried, on the edge of hysteria. "My children! Tell me what's become o' my young'uns, Brad! Don't keep me in the agony o' suspense. . . ."

Realizing that this was the moment he had both prayed for and dreaded, Brad drew a deep breath. "The smallpox, Lizzie . . . it struck our community hard. Didn't pass us by as we'd hoped and prayed."

She clawed at his sleeve. "My children, Brad! What about my young'uns! Tell me!" she insisted. "Lester—" She focused her attention on her firstborn. "How's my boy?"

"Lester's alive 'n' well . . . leastways, he's recovered enough 'til he's hankerin' to get back to his mules."

"Thank God." She fell back against the pillows again, drained of energy.

"An' Maylon?" she continued with her roll call. "How's Maylon? Did he get sick, too? Answer me!"

Brad took her hand, as if by doing so, he could pass his own strength on to Lizzie.

"Darlin' . . . Liz . . . I'm so sorry, but Maylon's . . . gone. Three weeks ago. I buried your boy myself. He died peaceful . . . and, I think, without pain. He just . . . slipped away from us—"

"Oh, my God—" Her groan was wrenched from the very depths of her soul, her loss no less because Maylon was the only one of her children not born to her.

"I miss him, too," Brad said softly. "But I can only guess how you're sufferin' . . . lovin' him since he was an infant in your arms—"

Lizzie struggled to swallow her tears, but another little sob slipped out along with her faint whisper, "Thad?"

Brad grinned in reply. "Eatin' everythin' that can't get up and run off!" he quipped. "He's gainin' ground the best o' the lot. I can tell he's feelin' pert these days, for he's as pesky as ever."

"Thank God," Lizzie sighed with relief before her eyes clouded once more. "A—an' Harmony?"

"She's fared better'n most. There'll be no scars to blight her beauty, you'll be happy to hear. . . ." Brad stalled for time, anticipating Lizzie's next question as she contemplated her wedding band, turning it loosely on her finger.

"Brad, tell me . . . Jem . . . he's better, too, ain't he? 'An gainin' strength by the day . . . jus' like all the others . . . 'cept Maylon?" Lizzie's voice was plaintive, and she could not bring her brimming eyes to meet Brad's sympathetic gaze.

Silence hung between them for a long moment, and Brad sensed that she already knew the answer.

"I did . . . the best I could, Lizzie."

"No! Oh, no!" Her moan was a keening wail, spilling from the wellspring of her sorrow. "Oh, Jem . . . Jem!" she sobbed, rocking herself as a mother rocks her child, seeking some solace in this primitive motion, but quickly spent, she gasped for breath, silently pleading with Brad to answer the questions she was too weak to ask.

Brad braced himself and measured his words carefully, knowing he must satisfy the sick woman's need to know about her dead husband's last moments, yet not tax her waning strength.

"I was with him to the end, Lizzie," Brad said gently. "An' in the instant before Jeremiah passed from this world to the next, he opened his eyes 'n' looked at me . . . 'n' I think he *knew* 'n' was ready to go. . . ."

Brad moved nearer the bed and took her hands in his. The tears were raining down her cheeks, yet she didn't make a sound.

"Thank you . . . Brad, for all you done," she gulped. "Without you . . . we'd have all died in our beds."

"Shhh," he said, wiping her wet cheek with a handkerchief he pulled from a back pocket. "I done no more'n you'd have done for me 'n' mine."

She sniffled and drew a quivering breath. "An'—an' how *are* your girls, Brad? Were they . . . spared?"

Brad shifted nervously, feeling an unnatural guilt over his

good fortune. "They're . . . well. Don't know why our household was passed over, but—"

"Praise God!" Lizzie mouthed the words. "Praise God—"

Brad paused, then plunged ahead. "There's one more, Lizzie—" He waited, gauging the effect of this last grim announcement. Seeing that she was fairly well composed, he continued. "It's Alton . . . Alton Wheeler's counted among the dead."

She winced as if suffering a physical blow. "Pa Wheeler . . . dead? But he always seemed so—"

It seemed silly to speak of Alton Wheeler as having seemed immortal, she realized suddenly, as if death could never touch him. Still, she'd always admired his spirit. Like one of his beloved Clydesdales, Alton Wheeler had been a powerful man, strong and stubborn, until the Lord tamed him and brought him under submission.

Even so, it wasn't easy to think of a life that no longer contained Pa Wheeler in it, and Lizzie wept in disbelief.

"I know," Brad whispered, patting her hand. "I know how you feel. When a man like Alton Wheeler passes on, it reminds a bloke of how brief a spell we spend on this earth . . . of how a body can go from livin' to dyin' in but the space of a heartbeat."

"We're born to die, my mama always said," Lizzie murmured and plucked absently at a stray thread on the coverlet as she wiped her tears. "She used to say that even the tiniest babe, the moment it comes squallin' out of its mama's body, begins to die to this world . . . that death is only the doorway to *real* life—"

"Your mama was a right smart woman."

"You'd have liked her."

"I know I would've," he said, "because . . . because a lot o' folks in the community have told me you're just like her. An' me 'n' mine . . . we're powerful fond o' you, Miss Lizzie. Fact is, we . . . love ya—"

"I–I know," Lizzie said and squeezed the hand holding hers. "And it'll be my loved ones who give me cause for findin' some scrap o' hope when the dark times of rememberin' come on me."

Softly at first, then with wrenching sobs, Lizzie began to cry. Brad arose, shaken, unsure how to proceed. He considered leaving the small room even as a part of him very much wanted to stay.

"Oh Brad," Lizzie sobbed. Her bony shoulders shook with the force of her weeping. "Oh, Brad!"

Taking his cue from her and knowing that never before had she so greatly needed a caring friend, he held out his arms to her and she wept against his chest until his shirt was wet with her tears. And still she cried.

That afternoon Lizzie mourned until Brad thought surely there were no more tears, but they continued to flood forth, seeming to purge her very soul, leaving her exhausted, until she fell asleep with her head pressed against his chest, her ear over the steady thud of his heart.

Gently he pried her from him, eased her back upon the pillow, tucked the coverlet up high, and tiptoed from the room.

"She knows," Brad informed Lizzie's youngsters when they gathered for the evening meal.

"We figured as much," Lester spoke for them.

There was a heavy silence as they waited respectfully, thinking of the great sorrow their mama was bearing, the loss they all had sustained.

"Umm . . . good soup, Harmony," Brad said.

"The boys helped. Thad chopped the meat, and Lester hauled up jars of vegetables from the cellar."

"Soon you'll all be well enough to manage on your own."
Lester's gaze swept the table as if he were collecting votes.
"We'll always need you, Brad . . . 'n' so will Mama."

"Don't worry, son," Brad said quietly. "I plan on bein' here
when she decides the time is right."

chapter
11

AFTER THE new year, even though Lizzie was up and about, working as her strength allowed, Brad stopped by often to check on the family. Though she was making a definite physical recovery, there was a downward cast to her lips and a melancholy look in her eyes that alerted Brad that all was not well.

"Liz, what's wrong? What's the matter?" Brad asked gently one day, intent on helping her share her burden, or even transfer it to his own broad shoulders if possible.

"Nothin' . . . I was just thinkin'," she sighed.

"Thinkin' about what?" he persisted.

"Lots o' things, I reckon," she said a bit evasively and nervously smoothed a wisp of hair from her cheek.

"Somethin' tells me you've got a partic'lar thought that keeps returnin' to plague you. What is it?"

She gave a startled laugh. "Reckon I do," she admitted. "Mama always said I was moody . . . thinkin' long thoughts for a country girl."

"That's not it," Brad said firmly, refusing to let her avoid facing the dark subject, whatever it was. "There's somethin' special troublin' you, Liz. An' I want to share your sorrows, same as I do your joys. Please let me. Let me know you . . . care . . . enough to share some o' your life with me."

Lizzie stopped her nervous pacing and sat down at the table. She poured two steaming cups of fresh, strong coffee. Brad measured a dollop of cream into hers just the way she liked it, then added sugar.

She gave him a tender look. "You're goin' to spoil me," she complained, taking a sip. "But it does make a body feel frightful pampered, drinkin' coffee so rich with cream 'n' sugar, don't it?"

"Liz-zie!" Brad warned in a playfully stern tone as for a second time she attempted to lead him off the track.

She gave a heavy, resigned sigh. "You know what's been troublin' me, Brad. There *have* been some grim thoughts layin' on my mind . . . Maylon . . . Jem . . . Pa Wheeler—"

"Somethin' tells me it's more'n your recent losses, Lizzie, sad as they was," Brad prompted.

She gave him a hard look. "You're a knowin' man, Brad Mathews. You seem to guess my thoughts almost 'fore I think 'em."

He nodded, spreading his hands. "Maybe it's 'cause I'm sensin' things in the woman I love."

"Maybe so—"

"What's upsettin' you, Lizzie? You can tell me true. I won't sit in judgment. An', if you'll let me, I'll share the burden with you or accept it as my own—"

"It—it's about Rory." Lizzie's lip trembled and she drew quick, shallow breaths. Then she exploded in a sob. When she managed to speak again, her voice was high and squeaky as she pinched her eyes shut and balled her hands until her knuckles grew white. "I miss him somethin' awful, Brad. It's like a livin' death, one that never ends . . . 'cause I was the one who drove him away—"

Brad rose abruptly, and rounded the corner of the table to lay both hands on Lizzie's shoulders. "I won't let you torment yourself this way, Liz. I saw Rory Preston leave Effingham County willin'ly. I saw him . . . 'n' the strumpet with him . . . with my own eyes—"

"No," Lizzie denied, sadly shaking her head, "Rory left out o' hurt, 'cause I lashed out at him in my own mis'ry. I said awful things, Brad—things my brother simply couldn't bear."

"The truth can be hard to take, but from what I hear tell, Lizzie, it was time he was told. Iffen you hadn't done it, I believe someone else would've."

"Maybe. Maybe not. Or maybe the teller would've been more charitable in the tellin'. But bein' as I was the one who done it, I regret more'n I can stand that I never had the chance to take back the cruel things I said. Or failin' to retract 'em, at least temper 'em later with words of forgiveness and love."

She lowered her face into her thin hands. "Oh, what must Rory have been thinkin' 'n' feelin' when I told my little brother to get out and never come back?!"

Brad patted Lizzie's shoulder absently, the way he might have comforted one of his daughters.

"Time is a fine healer, Lizzie," he pointed out. "It has a way of fadin' mem'ries. Like as not, Rory's already forgiven 'n' forgot."

Her eyes brightened with hope, then clouded with fresh anguish. "Then why didn't he answer my letters? Tell me that! Why? I wrote to him, long, long ago, back when Jeremiah first come outa his stupor 'n' you and Alton was helpin' him learn to walk again. I sent a passel o' letters—leastways, three or four of 'em—to the gold fields in Californy, since I reckoned that'd be the likeliest spot to catch up with him. . . ."

Brad was able to offer nothing more than a noncommittal shrug. "From what little contact I had with Rory, that would've been my guess, too."

"My fondest hope was that my little brother would write me back." Lizzie's eyes pooled with tears and she dabbed the moisture away with the corner of her apron. "I told him I loved him, Brad, said I was sorry for what passed between us. I even confessed that in my fury I was to blame for the fallin' out, too. Then I begged him to come home, or at least to let me hear news of him—"

"Then all I can say, Lizzie, is . . . give it time."

"But it's been *years!* And he never acknowledged my letters . . . none of 'em! I don't know if he's dead or alive, hardhearted or forgivin'. I've tried to put it from my mind, but I can't. It's drivin' me to distraction, Brad. When I laid in my sickbed, feelin' like I was a heartbeat away from dyin', I kept thinkin' of Rory, 'n' wonderin' why he was ignorin' me, his own sister—"

"I'm sure there's a good reason, Lizzie. Did you have your return address on your letters to Rory?"

Lizzie gave Brad a bald look. "Rory Preston knows exactly where I live," she said. "He don't need no return address."

Brad could not contain an amused smile as he ruffled her curly hair, then tenderly smoothed it from her cheek. He cupped her chin between his thumb and forefinger.

"But, Liz, your letters to him might never have reached 'im. Maybe the letters were one step behind Rory, with him movin' on in a hurry, lookin' to strike it rich. Unclaimed letters sent to Gen'ral Deliv'ry are returned to the sender after a spell," he explained.

Lizzie appeared as if she hardly dared hope. "Land sakes, I hadn't even thought of that!" she admitted in an awed tone, her eyes round with wonder. "I didn't have my return address on the envelopes 'cause the pencil warn't nothin' but a little stub as it was, and back then money was dear, so—"

"Try again then, Lizzie. Write Rory another letter . . . a dozen letters! Leastways, you'll have peace o' mind, knowin' you done all you could. An' if Rory's been gettin' and readin' your letters of apology and forgiveness, maybe this time they'll touch his heart and turn his thinkin' around . . . like the story in Scripture 'bout the widow woman and the judge. Keep after 'im, gal!" Brad encouraged.

"I'll do it!" she agreed. "Just as soon as I can find some paper."

"If you don't have writin' paper, I know Miss Linda would be pleased to offer some o' her best stationery for the cause. An' it goes without sayin' that we'll all be rememberin' you 'n' Rory in our prayers."

"There's so much to tell him," Lizzie mused. "So much sadness . . . oh, so much sadness—"

"An' don't forget the joy," Brad reminded her.

"Yes," Lizzie agreed, calling to mind the little daily blessings that at the time had seemed almost too insignificant to mention, but which, in retrospect, she knew to be the evidence of a loving and generous heavenly Father.

"An' when you write your brother, Liz, you might tell 'im 'bout us. Tell 'im there's a widower in the neighborhood who's hankerin' to marry you, the same feller as relieved 'im of the property he was in such a rush to get shed of. I reckon he'll remember me."

"Ah, Brad," Lizzie whispered, "it's true, ain't it?"

"That I love you? An' want to marry you? O' course. You've been doubtin' it?"

"Doubtin'?" Lizzie murmured dreamily. "Not for a minute. I just realized how true it is that all things work for good for those who love the Lord. Out of Rory's evil intent to sell Ma and Pa's property so's he could strike out on his own, came the great good of meetin' a man I've come to love enough to marry." She laid her fingers over Brad's warm hand resting on her shoulder. "A couple o' summers ago, you offered me a plumb thrillin' proposal, improper as it was then, with us thrashin' around, snagged tight by stickers in the blackberry patch—"

Brad blushed deeply and laughed. "The Lord helps those who help themselves!" he quipped. "An' I saw my chance to give Him a hand." He sobered, gazing down at her. "But it's no laughin' matter how much I love ya—"

"I love you, too, Brad. But—" She pulled away from him and cocked her head prettily. "—I shan't agree to marry you 'til I've received a proper 'n' romantic proposal."

Brad went down on one knee and cupped Lizzie's hand in his, looking into her face with a truly worshipful expression. When he spoke, his words were like sweet poetry.

"Yes ... oh, yes!" breathed Lizzie. "I'll be proud 'n' honored to be your bride, Brad."

"How soon?"

Lizzie's brow forked with concern. "Let me see," she said. "At this ripe ol' age, I'm not wantin' to miss out on a thing. Let's announce our betrothal, then you can court me, Mister Mathews. An' when a suitable length o' time has passed ... we'll be married. I—I think I'd like to be a June bride."

"I only want you to be happy, Liz," Brad said. "When should we announce our intentions?"

Lizzie giggled. "Reckon everybody 'n' his hounddog is aware of our intentions! But I kind of fancy Valentine's Day for makin' a formal 'nouncement. I've always been partial to the day made for lovers. 'Twas a fine Valentine's Day when Alton first realized he loved Miss Abby, 'member? I could

make cookies just like I did then. We could invite a few folks
to a Valentine's party ... then spring our news!"

Brad smiled. "Valentine's Day, it is, my love!"

After the long, sorrowful months, it felt good to laugh
again, Lizzie thought, with a burst of hope as her heavy
burdens lifted from her heart.

chapter
12

ON VALENTINE'S DAY Lizzie was up before dawn, preparing a hearty breakfast for her family, one that would stick to their ribs and fortify them for the long, cold walk to the schoolhouse, where Misses Linda Mathews and Katie Wheeler now instructed pupils in the Salt Creek School.

Scarcely had the door closed behind them than Lizzie dashed through the breakfast dishes. Once the kitchen was tidy, she got down the worn booklet in which she had penned hers and her mother's best receipts.

Thirty minutes later she was ready to roll out the first batch of heart-shaped sugar cookies. After they had cooled, she would ice them with frosting tinted with cherry juice, then edge them in snowy white piping.

Minutes after Lizzie removed the first pan of golden cookies from the oven and slid them onto a board covered with brown grocer's paper to cool, she looked up. Glancing out the window, she was surprised to see Brad ride by.

He waved cheerfully but made no move to rein in his horse. Lizzie could only conclude that he'd tarry a spell on his way back home and they'd complete their travel plans for the evening.

But she was far too busy to give Brad's strange behavior

another thought until that evening after supper when she was dressing for the Valentine's party. Looking into the mirror on her marble-topped dresser and noting that her cheeks were glowing, her pulse quickened with anticipation.

Tonight will be a night to remember, she thought happily, thinking of the response when she had casually invited a few of their close friends. Word of the social event had spread through the community like wildfire, and soon everyone was making plans to attend. With so many guests, Lizzie had asked for permission to hold the function in the schoolhouse, suggesting that each family bring a treat to help augment the evening's refreshments.

Now Lizzie's sugar cookies were carefully packed into a large graniteware pan and covered with a clean dishtowel after the frosting had hardened enough to prevent the cookies from sticking together.

"Brrr! It's gettin' colder out," Lester said as he came into the cabin, stamping snow off his boots. "I had to hold the bits in my bare hands to warm 'em before I stuck 'em into Mavis and Birdie's mouths. Pa always 'lowed as how it was a triflin' act an' only took a minute but was a major kindness as far as a horse or mule is concerned."

"You've hitched the mules to the wagon then?" Lizzie inquired, puzzled.

"Yes'm."

"But—"

"Miss Linda made a point of askin' me to, after she and Miss Katie dismissed class for the day," Lester explained hastily.

"I wonder whatever for—," Lizzie mused.

"So we'd get to the Valentine party tonight, Ma. We really ought to get on over there as soon as we can manage."

"But—but I'd really thought we'd be ridin' over with Brad 'n' his fam'ly."

"Miss Linda said her pa may be late."

"He was goin' somewhere today?" Lizzie inquired casually.

"Reckon so," Lester replied. "Miss Linda didn't say where, 'cept that it was pressin' business that couldn't wait another day."

"Oh, dear!"

What if a storm had blown in twelve miles to the north, and Brad would arrive at the party too late to make their announcement? Worse still, what if he did not get home at all? What if the horse slipped on the icy road and pinned him to the ground. . . ."

Lizzie forced herself to push the marauding thoughts from her mind. "We must get goin' then, darlin'!" She arose, smoothing her best frock into place as she reached for her Sunday-go-to-meetin' cloak.

"I'll carry the cookies, Ma," Thad offered.

Lizzie gave a chuckle. "Trust you not to let food get far from your sight, Thad Samuel."

"Did you save any for us to have here at home?"

"I sure did, Thad. The cookie jar's brimmin' full, and there's a canister of 'em down on the cellar steps, where they'll stay cool and crispy for a few more days."

Lester gave his mother a hand up into the wagon, boosted Harmony onto the straw piled in the back of the wagon, cautioning her to be careful where she put her feet, and instructed Thad to set the cookies down carefully. "An' mind you don't drop 'em, neither!" he warned his younger brother.

Keeping her disappointment in check, Lizzie forced a cheerfulness she didn't feel. "Maybe we should stop by the Mathews' farm. Iffen Brad ain't back from his . . . errand . . .

we wouldn't want his girls to miss out on the party for lack o' transportation."

"I was thinkin' along the same lines myself, Mama. It'll only take a jiffy. If their pa ain't home yet, I'm sure they'll be ready and waitin'."

Lester halted the mules and wagon in the side yard adjacent to the cabin. He approached the door, knocked, and a moment later Patricia Mathews appeared, and was joined by her sisters.

So preoccupied was Lizzie with her concern for Brad's safety and whereabouts that she paid scant attention to the conversation between Lester and the Mathews girls. She noticed only that when he gave instructions as to how they should be seated in the wagon, his voice was edged by an unaccustomed peevishness.

"Your father didn't make it back from his errand?" Lizzie asked.

She thought she saw the girls exchange veiled looks. But in the dim light cast by the lanterns attached to the mules' harnesses, she could not be certain.

"No'm," Jayne replied. "And he was settin' such store by goin' to this party, too."

"His business must have taken longer'n he planned," Rosalie said lightly.

"We can hope that he at least has a chance to make an appearance at the party tonight," Patricia remarked.

"Giddyap!" Lester cried, snapping the reins. And Lizzie wondered if she'd really heard a conspiratorial little laugh among Brad's daughters, or if the flurry of whispers was merely her own wishful thinking.

"See the fudge we made, Miss Lizzie?" said Jayne, extending a platter heaped with thick chocolate chunks that were heavy with lush black walnut meats.

"Looks delicious, girls," said Lizzie. "I'll be sure to sample a piece."

"And our mouths are waterin' for some of your sugar cookies," said Jayne graciously. "Nobody makes 'em like you do."

"Only my mama," Lizzie admitted, "and she's long gone. But I made plenty for everyone . . . even if my Thad's first in line!"

There was the sound of laughter and the call of cheerful greetings as those arriving for the party made their way from an array of wagons, buggies, and carts to stream into the schoolhouse that was growing warm as much from the congenial atmosphere of friends and neighbors as from the heat thrown out by the coal stove.

"My! Ain't this fun!" Lizzie cried as she looked around and saw one oldtimer enjoying a game of checkers with a young'un barely old enough to be in grade school.

Off in a corner, a bevy of giggling girls were playing "Pin the Tail on the Donkey." Another group of party-goers was caught up in a frenzied game of "Button, Button, Who's Got the Button?"

Each time the door opened to admit more revelers, Lizzie's gaze flew to the faces of the newcomers with keen anticipation, only to fall away in obvious disappointment when it was not Brad Mathews joining the merriment.

By half past eight, Lizzie had given up on his arriving in time for the festivities. So she no longer bothered to look up each time she heard the door rasp on its hinges and felt the blast of frigid air that momentarily tempered the almost cloying warmth of the large schoolroom.

"The band's gettin' ready to play!" Molly Wheeler told Marissa. "Maybe we'll have a real sing-along."

At the front of the room, several people Lizzie had barely

met gathered to make music. A young fellow began strumming his mandolin while another plucked the strings of a homemade banjo. To contribute background rhythm, a towheaded child shook a dried gourd, and an oldtimer, his white beard flapping, prepared to play the spoons.

"Mama, I—I hope you won't mind," began Lester, appearing at Lizzie's side, "but I brought Pa's . . . *my* . . . fiddle." He produced the instrument, unwrapping it from the burlap sack and brushing a blade or two of straw from its luminous, satiny surface.

"Lester!" Lizzie cried in a soft, surprised whisper.

His eyes, flooded with emotion, met hers, then flicked away. "Pa told me how Grandpappy Preston passed down the fiddle to him. An' he told me—before the mule kicked 'im—that iffen somethin' ever happened to 'im, the fiddle was mine. He taught me what he could, and I've been practicin' now 'n' again when I was alone in the cabin. I hope you don't mind—"

"Mind? O' course I don't mind. Jeremiah always intended for that fiddle to be yours, son. I just didn't know you had a hankerin' to play it." Lizzie's gaze was level and direct. "But I hope you know that in takin' up the bow, you're carryin' on the proud tradition handed down by the menfolk in our fam'ly."

"Pa said he thought I was right good, Ma," Lester went on, self-consciously scuffing the toe of his right brogan on the plank floor. "He said that, with hard work and dedication, I might even be as good as Grandpappy Will one day."

"There's no reason you shouldn't, darlin'. They're tunin' up now, Lester," Lizzie said, as tears of joy tingled to her eyes over this son of hers who was poised on the threshold of becoming a man after her heart—a responsible, God-fearing, clean-living man. "Go on up there and play extra special for your ol' ma!"

The rag-tag group of musicians held a huddled conference, then launched into their first tune. When it turned out not half-bad, they segued into a second melody with greater confidence, then a third. By the time they'd performed half a dozen numbers, they were playing with style.

"Heavens to Betsy!" Miss Abby complained to Lizzie when the entertainment was well underway. "Where can Alton be? The band's just not the same without him and his harmonica. I can't imagine where he's taken himself off to. Perhaps he'll be along presently to play with the others as he's always done."

"Miss Abby—" began a neighbor, aware of her confusion, then looked to the others for direction.

"Oh, you want *me* to play?" Alton's widow misunderstood. She offered a flustered smile and her pale fingers trailed to the lace at her collar. "I thank you for asking, but truly . . . I just couldn't. It wouldn't be fitting for a woman . . . in my condition . . . to appear so publicly. Indeed, I wouldn't have attended tonight at all, but our daughters just insisted I get out of the house for the evening. They vowed no one would blame me for a night's frivolity . . . even though . . . we're expecting our babe very soon now," she said, dropping her voice to a whisper.

Those who knew of the former schoolmarm's strange problem looked upon her with pity. Those who did not were puzzled, for it was plainly evident that Alton's widow had not been left in the family way after his passing. She was as thin as a rail.

"Have a piece o' fudge, Miss Abby," Lizzie invited and led her toward the refreshment table as the band struck up another song.

"I don't mind if I do," Abby agreed. "I'm eating for two these days, you know, though I don't want my wee one to be born with a sweet tooth. Do you believe a babe can be marked before birth, Lizzie?"

Before she could answer, the door opened, admitting a cold gust of wintry air, and the Mathews girls squealed in delight when their pa entered the schoolhouse.

Brad's cheeks were ruddy from the long, cold ride. Snow had sifted down to freeze on his collar, and his ears appeared half-frozen, but on his face was a smile to warm the heart even on this bitter-cold evening.

"Thank goodness, you're here at last!" Linda sighed, moving to greet him with a hug.

"We were prayin' you'd get here before it was too late!"

"Hurry, Pa! We've not told a soul 'bout your surprise," said Rosalie, "but if we have to keep the secret a moment longer, I think we'll all fairly burst!"

"Surprise? Secret?" The murmured words swept the room as the party-goers looked from one to the other in astonishment.

Brad shucked his coat and went over to stand by Lizzie. Drawing her to the front of the room, he boldly put his arm around her for all to see. "Miss Lizzie 'n' me wanted to take this occasion to make a happy announcement to you, our fam'lies and dear friends. We're plannin' on gettin' married, so we wanted y'all to witness our betrothal."

There was a gasp from among the women, random clapping from some of the men, then a burst of hearty applause.

Brad reached into his pocket. "And now for the surprise my girls were talkin' about—" He withdrew a velvet box and snapped back a tiny brass hasp, opening it to reveal an exquisite ruby ring, surrounded by a cluster of tiny diamonds.

"For you, Liz, to mark our engagement."

"An engagement ring?!" Lizzie cried, her mouth dropping open.

"Fresh from Sears, Roebuck and Company in Chicago!" Brad said proudly. "When I confided to my girls that we were plannin' on gettin' hitched come June, with the betrothal on Valentine's Day, they pressed me to make it a moment to remember. So they helped me choose a ring from the catalogue, and I ordered it posthaste. I've just come back from meetin' the train to take possession o' the order!"

With that, he slipped the ring on her finger.

"Oh, Brad . . . it's so . . . grand!" Her moist eyes sparkled with a sheen to rival the brilliance of the flashing stones. "I love it 'n' I love *you!*" she whispered. "But—but it must've cost you dear—"

"A triflin' price when compared to the value I place on your love, Lizzie."

With Brad at her side, it was as if the doubts from the early evening had never existed. Lizzie was almost dizzy from laughing and short of breath from talking by the time the party was over.

The Mathews girls giggled all the way home, teasing Lizzie about the look on her face when she saw the ring and her woebegone expression when she feared Brad might not be coming at all.

Lizzie turned to smile dreamily at Brad, who was riding his saddle mare alongside the wagon as Lester guided Birdie and Mavis home, dropping off Brad's daughters on the way.

At their place, Lester rubbed down the mules and turned them into the barn lot for the night, while Thad and Harmony scampered into the house and prepared for bed.

Lizzie poured Brad a cup of coffee, then one for herself. Settling down at the kitchen table, they talked quietly until

Lester came in from the barn, bade them a good-night, and retired to his attic room.

"I must be goin' home soon," Brad said at last. "But the time's comin' when I won't have to leave a'tall."

"I know," said Lizzie with a sigh, "an' while it may be shameless o' me to admit it, I'm keenly anticipatin' that date."

"Ah . . . no more'n I," Brad murmured. "I'm afraid I'm a mighty impatient man, darlin'. The time's goin' to drag, I fear . . . a whole season afore I can make you mine."

Lizzie laid her hand against his cheek and gave him a misty smile. "Time will pass quickly," she predicted, "for we've much to do."

"I'm figgerin' on loggin' some trees from my property, haulin' 'em to the sawyer's, and havin' enough timber to construct a fine addition to your cabin so's we can all live together in comfort come June."

"I'd counted on as much. An' that'll take time."

"I wish it warn't such a far piece to haul logs to the sawyer."

"Yes, 'tis a pity," Lizzie murmured. "Harm and Pa used to wish we had a mill close by, too."

The couple talked on in low tones, planning and dreaming, as Lizzie continued to steal enraptured glances at the engagement ring sparkling on her finger. How blessed she was with the love of this good and generous man, she thought, and more than that, with his four daughters who, instead of resenting her intrusion into their lives, had seen fit to welcome her warmly.

"Brrr! It's gettin' colder by the minute," she said at the door when Brad was ready to leave. "You'll freeze on the way home." She snugged his collar up around his neck and gave his scarf an extra tug.

"Not if you give me a kiss to keep me warm," he murmured.

"Why, I declare!" Lizzie said, blushing when she considered how long it had been since she'd been kissed by a man. Not since that interlude in the blackberry patch, when Brad, overcome by emotion, had asked her to put aside poor Jeremiah and marry him, even though it meant that a sacred promise would be broken.

"It's no longer scand'lous, Lizzie," he chided. "We're promised to one 'nother."

"I know. It's just that—"

Not waiting for her argument, Brad lowered his lips to hers as he claimed what was now his due.

"Sweet," he said when Lizzie's lips left his. "Even sweeter than I remembered."

"Will that help keep you warm as you're headin' on home?" Lizzie teased, her eyes dancing as she bestowed another quick kiss on Brad's soft lips that curved into a smile as he gazed down at her.

"It will warm my thoughts tomorrow . . . 'n' next week . . . 'n' next month . . . 'til the weddin' day itself. But it also whets my appetite for more."

Lizzie gave him a loving shove to where his patient mare awaited him. "Begone with you, Brad Mathews! June will be here afore we know it, and I'll become your blushin' bride, just like in the penny dreadful novels."

"I b'lieve the ladies in those novels are deservin' of a gen-u-ine honeymoon, ain't they?" Brad questioned, turning back to regard her in the pale light streaming from the window.

"Brad . . . what're you sayin'?" How many more surprises did he have up his sleeve, she wondered.

"Only that you shall have a honeymoon, too, Lizzie," he promised.

"But, Brad . . . the ring, a honeymoon . . . all o' that's

uncommon costly. And there are so many things we need 'round the farm—"

"Ah, Lizzie, neither of us is in the springtime o' our youth. We've shouldered some heavy burdens in our time, known toil 'n' trouble. We know what it's like to sacrifice for others and see denial as a way o' life. Pray God, woman, that when we wed, 'tis the last time for both o' us. And believin' we'll grow old together, it's our last chance to have a weddin' 'n' a life ... that's fittin'ly romantic."

"Brad ... Oh, Brad ... You do understand my silly notions, don't ya?"

He nodded. "Hardly silly, Liz, when I feel such romantic stirrin's myself."

Then, before she could stop herself, Lizzie was in Brad's arms, kissing him with love, appreciation, and a thousand wondrous emotions.

When Brad Mathews disappeared into the dark night, Lizzie truly knew what it was to hope for the morrow and looked toward the coming days with sweet anticipation.

chapter
13

ON HER WEDDING day, Lizzie felt young again, as young as she'd felt the day she pledged her vows to Harm Childers, as young as the day she'd vowed to love Jeremiah Stone forever and ever.

Now both men were lying beneath the sod, and the Lord had seen fit to reward her with the love of another good man. Somehow this time, she thought, she and Brad Mathews, now in the rich, ripe summer of their years, would live to grow old together. It was this hope that put a twinkle in her eyes this fair June day and lent a radiance to her countenance that fairly took Brad's breath away when he saw his bride.

When Lizzie came down the aisle of the little white church, she was wearing a dress created especially for the day by a seamstress in Effingham and a millinery masterpiece fashioned by a hatmaker in Watson. It was a costume and a day unlike any the good folks of Salt Creek had ever seen before.

And the ceremony itself, conducted by the visiting parson, was not the last of the surprises. Following the reception set up on plank tables in the churchyard, a blushing Lizzie turned her young'uns over to Lemont Gartner's care, as did Brad, instructing his girls to get settled, in his absence, in their new quarters tacked onto Lizzie's cabin.

"If there's a need to contact us, we'll be at the Benwood Hotel in Effingham," Brad informed Lemont. "Barrin' misfortune, we'll be home in four or five days. This'll be the first vacation for Lizzie 'n' me, so we're goin' to take our ease and see what there is to see in the county seat."

"Don't worry none 'bout your young'uns. They couldn't be in better hands . . . the Lord's 'n' mine," Lemont said with a gleam in his eye. "Now, be off with you!" And he gave one of Brad's horses a smart slap on the rump and waved as the newlyweds were borne away down the road toward their future.

Brad left the rig at the livery stable and escorted Lizzie to a towering brick building on Jefferson Avenue. Inside the hotel, Lizzie stared in awe, drinking in the sights that greeted her—rich carpets, gleaming hardwood floors, overstuffed furniture, snowy linens, crystal chandeliers.

"Brad, this is like a dream," she said as they registered with the clerk behind the counter.

"For once, Lizzie Mathews, we're goin' to know somethin' more'n worry, responsibility, and hard work. We're goin' to savor life in the lap o' luxury!"

"Just bein' all alone with you Brad, is luxury enough."

Brad's hand felt for hers as he signed the guest register: *Mr. and Mrs. Bradley Mathews, Watson, Illinois.*

And as Lizzie was assisted up the stairs by her new husband, who followed behind the hotel employee bearing their bags, she knew that she would never forget the utter happiness of that moment, no matter what trials and tribulations they might one day be called upon to face.

Lizzie rolled over and blinked her eyes open. In the faint light of dawn, she took in the unfamiliar room—its vaulted ceiling, the delicate flowered wallpaper, the rich, dark wainscoting. It was all true . . . it wasn't a fleeting dream. She was really here in this fairytale place with the man she loved.

They had spent three wonderful days, strolling the streets of the town, holding hands as they peeked in the impressive store windows at displays of outrageous fashions and bric-a-brac, the likes of which Lizzie had never seen in all her born days. They had picnicked in the park. They had indulged themselves in fine meals served in the hotel dining room, complete with candlelight and bouquets of fresh flowers on every table.

All this Lizzie recalled as she lay in her bed beside Brad. Then, thinking of the children they'd left at home, a strange, lonely longing set in.

"Brad?"

"Ummmm?" he mumbled an answer as he drifted toward wakefulness.

Lizzie traced the curve of his cheek, trailing her fingertip over his lip. He opened his eyes and grinned at her.

"Mornin', Missus Mathews!"

"Another fine day we're havin', Mister Mathews!"

"And what would you be wantin' us to do today?" Brad asked. "We could take a walk down the avenue again, or order a picnic luncheon from the hotel kitchen and laze in the park, or—"

Lizzie's expression grew serious. "No doubt you're goin' to think I'm daft for sure, Brad, but I don't want to go on a picnic. I can do that at home. To tell you true . . . I'd like to see my young'uns. I'm missin' our children somethin' awful."

"I'll be forthright, Liz. I thought of the children more'n a time or two myself durin' the night."

"I know we'd planned on stayin' in town for another day," Lizzie began in a tentative tone, "an' I am havin' a good time, but would you consider me downright ungrateful and be too sorely disappointed if we departed for home today?"

Brad set his feet to the floor. "Not a'tall, darlin'. Fact is, I'm not accustomed to livin' a life o' leisure, an' I'm missin' my work same as I'm missin' the children."

Lizzie sighed. "I thought it'd be heaven on earth to eat meals prepared by others' hands, with them doin' up the dishes when the table's cleared. But I find I'm missin' my chores 'round the house, too."

Lizzie and Brad bounded out of bed and reached for their street clothes.

"Iffen we hurry, we can be home afore noon," Brad declared. "We'll leave just as soon as we've had our breakfast and bought some candy sticks for the young'uns."

After a final, extravagant breakfast in the hotel dining room, Brad escorted Lizzie to their room and left her there while he went to fetch the horses and buggy from the livery stable. Meanwhile, Lizzie packed their valise, then checked the room for any forgotten belongings before carrying their baggage downstairs and setting it in the lobby.

Since Brad had not yet appeared with the rig, Lizzie stepped outside for a bit of fresh air. She smiled cheerfully at passersby as they passed by the Benwood Hotel on their way to do business at other nearby establishments.

Suddenly, Lizzie's lips parted with surprise when she saw a slim, blond woman leaving the baker's shop. The woman looked, for all the world, like Miss Abby! And when the woman gave Lizzie a perplexed look, there was no mistaking her identity.

"Miss Abby! Miss Abby!"

The woman turned as if from some long instilled instinct. But she looked at her old friend without so much as a flicker of recognition even when Lizzie clutched Abby's arm and drew her around until they were standing face-to-face.

"What are you doin' here, Miss Abby?" Lizzie asked, her voice growing shrill with alarm. "How did you get to Effingham? Surely you know me—Lizzie! Lizzie Stone . . . I mean, Lizzie *Mathews* now," she explained, realizing that her words were making little sense to the woman, even though she had attended the wedding with the Wheeler girls only days before.

"Excuse me . . . have we met?" Abby asked, peering at her intently.

Lizzie gripped the demented woman's elbow and pulled her from the flow of the crowd on the main street of town. "Miss Abby, you're a long ways from home. What are you doin' here?"

Abby frowned thoughtfully. "Why . . . I don't know. Waiting for Alton, I suppose. Yes, that's it. I'm waiting for my husband. Now, where do you suppose he can be? That man—" She sounded irked. "He's taken to disappearing these days. It's gotten to the point where sometimes I swear he's never around at all. And that's hardly appropriate behavior from a man whose poor wife is in the motherly condition and could use a bit more coddling and husbandly concern."

Lizzie groaned and twisted the fabric of her new dress in her hands as she twirled around, searching the street for Brad or the Wheeler girls. But there was not a soul she recognized in sight.

"Miss Abby, please. Think hard. How did you get to Effingham?"

"Did *you* bring me here?" Miss Abigail asked, responding as if she might have hit on the answer to a riddle.

Lizzie sighed with exasperation. "Are the girls with you?"

"They're with their pa. Alton adores his girls, you know."

She knit her brows. "I do hope he'll be as doting a pa to our wee one when it gets here."

"Did Miss Molly handle the horses and drive you here?"

"The horses? Oh . . . the horses. Yes . . . horses . . . horses," Abby murmured without comprehension.

"Doc and Dan . . . where are they?" Lizzie cried, her cheeks heating when she became aware of the peculiar looks they were drawing from interested bystanders.

"My goodness. I—I think . . . oh, yes, now I remember the horses. Some . . . man . . . took them."

"At the livery?" Lizzie asked, feeling a flicker of relief before she realized it might be premature to believe the horses were in the proper hands. "What did you do with the horses, Miss Abby? Where are they? Did you take them to the livery stable?" She articulated her words loudly as if Miss Abby were either a very small child or very deaf!

"I told you! A man . . . a man . . . a man—," she replied in a sing-songy manner. "A man took them."

"Thunderation!" Lizzie exploded in aggravation. "Listen, you're stayin' with me until we figger this out. Brad should be here any minute now."

"Brad?" Abby inquired politely as if she'd never heard the name before.

"Lord in heaven, give us strength and patience to deal with what we're about to face," Lizzie muttered under her breath, but aloud she said, "I wonder what's keepin' Brad?"

Almost no sooner had she spoken his name than her husband appeared with the horses and buggy.

"Miss Abby! What a surprise," he remarked. "Where're the girls? It's a tad early to be in town, ain't it? You must've left home before the cock crowed."

Miss Abby stared at him in confusion, then she turned to

Lizzie as if seeking guidance as to the identity of the strange man accosting her.

"I don't know how she got here," Lizzie explained to Brad, ignoring the woman's unspoken plea. "An' she don't know where the girls are, where the horses are, nothin'!"

"But surely she didn't walk all the way to Effingham."

Lizzie shrugged. "Ain't got no clue how she got here. But land sakes, we can't let her wander 'round town like this, an' I'm a little surprised . . . and put out with the Wheeler girls . . . if they brung her to town, then left her on her own."

Brad's lips thinned in a tight line. "I don't think we'll find the Wheeler girls in Effingham, but we'll have to take a jaunt through town and keep an eye out for 'em afore we strike out for home with Miss Abby in our charge."

They drove slowly, craning their necks, searching the streets and avenues for a sign of Doc, Dan, and the Wheeler girls. From one end to the other they drove, scouring the length and breadth of the town.

"We've looked everywhere," Lizzie said at last. "They're just not here."

"If Miss Abby's wandered off, the girls must be wild with worry."

"Then let's hurry home."

En route for Salt Creek, a dark cloud of worry settled over them like a pall, and they drove in silence, their thoughts tumbling. Lizzie and Brad had quickly learned that it was pointless to question poor Miss Abby. Her answers were vague and misleading, and when they persisted, she bristled in indignation.

Pulling up into the Wheelers' yard, Brad hailed the cabin, and the three Wheeler girls rushed outside to greet the new arrivals, stark relief etched into their features.

"Mama! Where on earth have you been?" asked Mary Katharine.

"Where are Doc and Dan?" Molly gasped.

"The wagon!" Marissa cried. "Where is it? We've been stranded a-foot for days!"

As Alton's daughters clustered around Brad's wagon, assaulting Abby with their questions, she regarded them with a dazed, stony stare. One after another, mute tears trickled down her cheeks.

Mary Katharine was upset, touched by her stepmother's plight.

Marissa was angry.

But Molly was resigned. And it was she who began the lengthy explanation of Miss Abby's whereabouts over the past few days. "Mama took the team and went to see the doctor the day before yesterday," she began. "I offered to drive her . . . in fact, I practically insisted on it . . . but she had a bee in her bonnet that she was goin' to go by herself. Mama has her moments of bein' plumb unreasonable."

"Fool! You shouldn't have let her go alone," Marissa blurted, turning on her twin. "She's not competent 'n' maybe you aren't, either!"

Molly recoiled as if she'd been slapped. "Then try stoppin' her yourself if you're so smart!"

Marissa tossed back her dark hair and cast them a defiant, determined look. "I would've stopped her . . . if I'd had to use a loggin' chain to do it!"

Molly was aghast. "'Rissa, you wouldn't! She's a human bein'! She's the only mama we've ever known—"

"She's a dad-blasted burden, that's what she is!"

"And you're a selfish, foul-tempered snip!"

"While you're a lily-livered, nasty-nice, goody-two-shoes!"

"Girls! Stop it this instant!" Katie cried.

"Mary Katharine's right. You two hush up right now," ordered Brad.

"Lord have mercy—," whispered Lizzie.

"What're we going to do now?" Katie moaned, turning to Brad.

"The boys 'n' I'll go in to town and see if we can piece together what's transpired 'n' what's become o' the horses."

"Miss Abby's so batty, she probably abandoned them," Marissa hissed uncharitably. "Poor Pa must be rollin' over in his grave."

"Hush your mouth!" Molly said sharply. "You act like Mama is doin' this because she wants to vex us."

"She's no mother of *mine*."

"Girls, bickering amongst ourselves will accomplish nothing," Katie intervened. "If Mama abandoned the horses, we have no real cause for alarm. Doc and Dan are old and gentle. They won't damage anybody's property. And, as well-known as Pa's team is in these parts, there's a good chance someone could come riding in at any minute, leading our team home to us."

"We can sure hope so," Brad agreed, though he doubted it.

After entrusting Abby into her stepdaughters' care, Brad and Lizzie set out for home.

"I don't like this a'tall," Lizzie broke the burgeoning silence.

"Me neither, sweetheart. An', deep down inside, I have a hunch we're goin' to like it a lot less afore we finally get to the bottom o' things."

Upon their arrival at home, everyone rushed out to greet them. Lemont followed in the young'uns wake, offering assurances that everything had progressed fine and dandy since the newlyweds had departed for Effingham. But when he saw the looks on the faces of his friends, he knew they must have encountered serious problems somewhere along the way.

Hastily Brad explained the circumstances to the young folks, and the atmosphere grew heavy as they silently reflected upon the possibilities.

"Boys, we'd better make a trip to town. Lemont? Care to join us?"

The older man nodded. "Count me in. Findin' out what's become o' Al's team seems to be the main worry at the moment."

Brad patted Lizzie's hand. "Hold supper for us, darlin'. Dunno when we'll be back."

"Brad, I know you've got a lot on your mind. But could you duck into the postal office in Watson iffen you go that way, 'n' see if we've got any mail?"

"Sure thing," he said softly, knowing how badly she wanted to hear from her brother. "Consider it done."

The evening hours dragged by. Lizzie's nerves were frayed and raw by the time the group returned well after dark.

Mute, they filed into the cabin.

Brad's eyes were dull, his lips compressed in a tight line.

Lester looked as if he wanted to weep.

Thad was obviously disgusted.

Lemont seemed shaken, his shoulders sagging.

"Well?" Lizzie waited for someone to speak.

"She sold 'em!" Thad spat.

"*Sold* Doc and Dan? No, that's not right, Ma, she *gave* 'em away!" Lester yelped indignantly.

"Got shed of the whole shebang—two good horses 'n' a stout wagon—for a niggardly five dollars." Lemont's round face was florid with emotion.

"What's done is done, fellers," Brad said with resignation

and dropped into a chair around the table as the others followed suit.

"Five dollars!" Lizzie gasped, numb.

"The woman's plumb crazy!" Thad exploded.

"Son—" The lone word was a rebuke.

"Mind your mother, boy, 'n' keep a civil tongue in your head," corrected Brad. "That's no way to speak o' Miss Abby, regardless of what's been done. Poor woman's not accountable. She doesn't know what she's doin' these days, and hain't for a good long time."

"What happened?" Lizzie asked, almost dreading the answer.

Brad leaned forward, arms on the table, shoulders hunched. "We heard that Amos O'Toole's been drivin' Alton's team 'n' wagon, so we paid a call on Mister O'Toole. Turns out that rumor was true. He had the team in his possession. The rotter took terr'ble advantage of Miss Abby."

"H—he's no better'n a horse thief," Lemont sputtered.

"Regardless of our feelin's about the deal," Brad went on, "the Clydesdales are now his. If he can live with what he's done, the Wheeler girls'll have to do without transportation."

"We trailed Miss Abby's actions, Ma," Lester put in. "She took the train to Effingham. That's how she happened to be wanderin' around when you found her this mornin'."

"Has she any money left . . . leastways, enough to apply against a horse 'n' wagon to ease the girls' loss a bit?" Lizzie inquired.

She was chilled by Brad's harsh laugh.

"As addlepated as poor Miss Abby is, I doubt it. We'll have no choice but to scrape up the funds to purchase a horse 'n' conveyance. But 'long with that will go strict orders that the girls are not to let their stepmama go anywhere unchaperoned."

"I think they'll be keepin' a sharp eye on Miss Abby from now on."

"I hate to admit it, Liz, but the day may come when they'll have to lock 'er up to keep 'er safe an' protect themselves as well."

The idea of the once intelligent, gentle schoolteacher— Alton's beloved wife—being imprisoned in her own home, was enough to freeze Lizzie's heart. "God forbid it should ever come to that! The poor woman needs our prayers."

"She's got 'em," Brad assured her. "But she'll get compassionate supervision, as well."

chapter
14

FOR THE REST of the summer, late afternoons and weekends found Lizzie's family bending their energies toward preserving foodstuffs for the coming winter and adjusting to living together as one big family.

Brad pastured some livestock at his farm, allowing cattle and a few mules to graze the hilly woodlands. Chickens, hogs, and the majority of the farm animals were confined on Lizzie's acreage, remaining under his watchful care.

The house where Lizzie and Rory had been reared, the house that had sheltered the Will Preston family and later Brad and his girls was woefully empty, but it served as a site to store the goods that overflowed the cabin where they all now resided in gregarious harmony.

And the cycle of the seasons rolled on. Summer gave way to fall . . . Autumn relinquished to winter . . . Winter gales bowed to the gentle spring breezes, to be replaced once more by summer's blistering heat.

For Lizzie, what had been a long stretch of uninterrupted bliss was shattered when problems seemed almost to be borne on the hot, dry winds.

It was nearing the Fourth of July when Katie Wheeler drew near Lizzie and Brad's farm, racing the aged mare Brad had given the girls over the rough, rutted roads. The decrepit old wagon jounced mercilessly over the packed clay, and the thud and bang of the wooden wheels did not drown out her screams that rose above the din and flying dust.

"Brad! Lizzie! It's Mama! Please . . . help—"

Running to the side yard, Brad caught the harness as the horse bolted out of control. Brad was jerked along for a pace or two but managed to slow the animal as the wagon clattered to a halt.

Katie dropped the reins and buried her face in her trembling hands. When Lizzie ran from the cabin, the girl tumbled from the wagon into her arms. In a state of shock, Katie was able only to stammer a few nearly incoherent sentences.

"Pull yourself together now!" Lizzie ordered sternly as she fumbled in the pocket of her apron for a linen handkerchief that she pressed into the hysterical girl's hands. "Is it Miss Abby?"

"Yes! And men—horrible, awful men!" Katie gasped, shivering in terror. "One of them even pointed a gun at us! Mama and the girls are locked . . . in the house." She drew a shuddering breath. "I–I managed to sneak away and hitch the horse to the wagon before they saw me. Thank God I got away . . . before they missed me. Oh, Miss Lizzie, what'll we do?"

Inwardly, Lizzie quailed. "You poor darlin'," she crooned and folded the quaking girl to her.

Brad laid a comforting but firm hand on Katie's shoulder. "Calm down a little, then tell us what happened but make it quick. From the sound of it, there's no time to waste."

Katie drew a deep, ragged breath, mopped her forehead with the hankie Lizzie had given her, and proceeded to launch an explanation. "Molly drove Mama in to Effingham earlier this week. She said she was going to consult the doctor there. You know how Mama can wheedle and persuade over her . . . medical problems. Molly let Mama out at the doctor's home and then left to water the horse at the livery stable. She wasn't gone more than half an hour, she said, and drove the wagon back to the doctor's residence and parked in a shady spot to wait. But Mama failed to come out. When Molly went in to inquire . . . she found out that Mama hadn't consulted with the doctor at all!"

"Horsefeathers!" Lizzie said. "Miss Abby's gettin' plumb sly for a woman who was once so open 'n' trustworthy."

"What happened then?" Brad pressed.

"Quite naturally, poor Molly was in a stew. She traversed the town, inquiring of folks she happened to meet if they'd seen a woman matching our mama's description. Finally she found her. She was rambling . . . an—and her purse was filled with money, though she declared she didn't know where it came from. There were over a hundred one- and five-dollar bills!"

"Where did Miss Abby get all that money?" Brad asked, frowning. "That's a lot o' jack to be carryin' around."

"That's what we tried to figure out," Katie admitted. "But you know how Mama's been lately. The more we questioned her, no matter how gentle we were, the more confused and abrasive she got. When it dawned on her that maybe she'd done something wrong, she started weeping, and she's been in an absolute state of collapse ever since."

"Then you still don't know where the money came from?" Brad asked before Lizzie got a chance to.

Katie gave a short, bitter laugh. "Oh, yes. We found out minutes before I sneaked away in a panic. It seems that Mama sold the farm to those crude, ill-mannered men who came to take possession of their property!"

"*What?!*" Brad and Lizzie cried in unison.

"She sold the farm," Katie said in a dull tone, "just as she did Doc and Dan—"

"God in heaven, no!" Brad moaned.

Fresh tears brimmed in Katie's eyes. "And now th—those men . . . they're ordering us to get out," she said and began to sob. "What are we going to do? It's the only home we've ever known . . . and I don't know where we'll go! My poor mama . . . my poor sisters—" She broke into a fit of weeping and could not go on.

"We'd best get over there right away," Brad said. "Hitch up the horses, Les!" he called out, and the youth who'd been standing nearby, close enough to have overheard at least part of Katie Wheeler's sad soliloquy, flew out the door and brought the team around.

Brad boosted Katie to the wagon. Not bothering to wait for a hand up, Lizzie flung herself aboard. Then Brad leapt to the seat beside her and lashed the horses with the reins, with Lester hopping on as the wagon pulled away.

A short while later, when Brad slowed the team to negotiate the turn into the lane leading to the Wheeler cabin, the first thing he saw was the sight of some unfamiliar saddle horses tethered to a sapling that was growing in the fencerow. Two rough-looking men lounged in the shade of the lilac bush that had long since lost its blooms. At his approach they stiffened, drew to attention, and regarded the arrivals warily, like cur dogs with their hackles rising.

"We come in peace," Brad said quietly, "to find out what business brings you to the Wheeler farm."

"'Tain't the Wheeler farm no more," the taller one taunted, grinning to reveal rotting teeth stained by tobacco. "It's our'n. We've got the papers to prove it." He patted his leather vest, slick with sweat and the grease from spilled foodstuffs.

Lizzie felt her stomach turn over. Beside her, Katie seemed to wilt.

"Buck up!" ordered Lizzie under her breath, speaking to herself as much as to Katie. "Now's no time to faint dead away. Pray! An' call on the protection of the Lord!"

"Where's your proof?" Brad asked, dismounting and stepping boldly and confidently toward the pair.

The shorter one gestured in the direction of the cabin. "That yaller-haired woman sold it to us—fair 'n' square—the other day when she was amblin' around town, approachin' folks on the street like a beggar woman."

"Oh, no!" Lizzie whispered. "Poor Abby!"

"She 'lowed as how she was wantin' to raise money to buy her young'uns some Christmas presents," said his partner. "Reckon she was gettin' an early start on playin' Santy Claus."

The shorter man guffawed. "Well, sir, quite natural-like, we asked what she had of value to sell."

The taller fellow gave Brad a bawdy look. "We's figgerin', y'see, that maybe she was offerin' herself, 'n' her not a bad-lookin' woman at that. But to our surprise, she told us 'bout a plot of land—this here farm—that she was willin' to sell. We asked what she'd take for it. She told us to make 'er an offer."

"So we did," the other said, "and hot darn if she didn't take us up on it!"

"We'd been lucky in poker, so our pockets was stuffed with jack. We give her most of the day's winnin's, and she deeded us this farm. We took the little lady by the Effingham Title Company afore she could change her mind, so it's nice 'n' legal."

"May be legal. But it ain't right."

The pair hooted as if only a hayseed farmer would set store by such backwoodsy ethics.

"Well, in case you're thinkin' of contestin' the deal," the tall

143

one warned, "we have a passel o' witnesses who'll state she was in her right mind that day 'n' has only gone to pieces since she done it. Y'all don't stand a chance. So you may's well start reconcilin' yourself to the fact that your loss is our gain! This here is our land—'n' a nice spread it is, too!" Giving Brad a sidelong glance, he spat on the ground, narrowly missing the toe of Brad's worn boots. "Fact is, we want the woman 'n' her young'uns off our place."

Somehow Brad remained unruffled. "But Missus Wheeler 'n' her girls . . . well, they have no place to go. She's a widow woman, 'n' she's not been . . . herself . . . in quite a spell. Please," he begged on his neighbors' behalf, "if you've any decency a'tall, sell the farm back to 'er for what you paid."

The men exchanged a look through slitted lids, found themselves in agreement, and shook their heads slowly, irritatingly so.

Lizzie squirmed on the wagon seat, fairly itching to smack the snide smiles from their faces. Instead, she wrung her hands in despair while poor Katie shrank beside her.

A second stream of brown tobacco juice followed the first, landing even closer to Brad's other boot. "Then she should've thought o' that earlier," said the shorter man. "She shouldn't have been so eager to sell off her farm if she didn't wantta leave."

"But the woman's not competent, I tell you!" Brad flared. "She didn't know what she was doin'."

"We have plenty o' witnesses in the saloon who'll swear dif'rent."

Brad's expression was one of contempt. "I'll just bet you do!" His next words raked the air like a whiplash. "I hope you'll live to know the grief you've caused this fam'ly . . . or repent o' your evil deed 'n' get right with the good Lord!"

The pair shrugged. Obviously, repentance was not in their plans.

"You can move the lady out, mister," said the taller one with a sneer, "or I'm afeared we'll have to do the honors."

Brad leveled them a withering look before his shoulders sagged. "Then give me 'til nightfall."

The men thought it over, then gave a grudging nod. "All right. But hurry! We ain't got all day!"

Peering out of the cabin, their faces pale and drawn, the Wheeler girls heard the verdict and scurried about to pack while Lester remained behind to offer assistance and a semblance of manly protection.

When the first load was ready to roll, with Miss Abby tucked between them, Brad and Lizzie urged the horses on and they started for home at a brisk trot.

"This is a pretty kettle o' fish," Brad said when they were underway.

"I'm beyond bein' amazed by anything Abby does any more," Lizzie said. "It'd been peaceable for so long, though, I reckon I didn't think she'd go off again, given the chance. No doubt the girls had let down their guard, too."

"If it's any consolation, Liz, there ain't much ruination left for her to do. I'm plumb sick about it."

"Me, too. And Marissa Wheeler was spittin' tacks . . . not that I can really blame her. And she does have Alton's temper . . . leastways, the kind he had before he committed his life to the Lord."

"Poor Molly. Folks say that girl's so much like Alton's first wife, Sue Ellen—bearin' whatever she must in silence 'n' keepin' her own counsel. But it was clear as cut glass that she was heartbroke," Brad ventured.

Lizzie sighed. "An' Katie's so worried she can't think straight."

Brad gave her a look of alarm. "I, for one, am thinkin' she has a perfect right to be! Did you see the way Marissa was smilin' at those men—the very rogues who were turnin' her and her ma and sisters out of their home? When we arrived, she was mad as a wet hen, but before we'd stowed the final trunk on this load, I caught her watchin' 'em 'n' smilin'!"

"No!"

"'Fraid so. Thought maybe you'd seen it, too, 'n' were preparin' to rebuke the girl."

"I most certainly would've! She'd have thought she was facin' the wrath o' God by the time I finished with her—"

"Alton would've bent her over his knee. The idea of a God-fearin' girl havin' the audacity to act like a common strumpet! I probab'ly should've done somethin' on the spot. But I had my hands full at the time. Besides, I feared it'd be two young blokes—'n' them bearin' shootin' irons—agin one middle-aged man 'n' boy."

"Don't fault yourself, Brad. You done all you could. But I'll speak to Marissa. That girl does worry me."

"What're we goin' to do, Lizzie?" Brad changed the topic. "It's true the Wheelers don't have no place to go, but we can't hang 'em on pegs at our place. Even with the new addition, the house is brimmin' with our own young'uns—"

As an idea struck, Lizzie turned to regard her husband over Abby's shoulder. She started to laugh. Lightly at first, then harder until the sound of her mirth echoed across the tumbling hills.

The nettled glance Brad gave her indicated that he clearly found the situation anything but funny.

"Have you forgotten?" she asked. "Our own house may be fairly bustin' at the seams. But Mama's cabin—your old house, Brad . . . it's empty now, ain't it? They can live there, can't they?"

146

He groaned, slapping his forehead with the heel of his hand. Then he, too, began to laugh, uneasily at first, then in great whooping bursts as relief washed over him and the tension drained away.

He looked at Miss Abby, who sat between them, still as an alabaster statuette.

"Reckon I can't fault Miss Abby's addlepatedness when it's plain that my own thinkin's none too reliable this day," he confessed with a wry grin.

Lizzie surveyed the woman who showed no indication that she comprehended her surroundings at all. A prickle of alarm crept along her spine at the prospect of the future.

"What are we goin' to do with her, Brad? How are we goin' to control her? She's a trial to the girls . . . an' more'n that, she may soon be a danger to herself."

"First off, we're goin' to have to forget that Miss Abby is a woman grown. We'll need to treat 'er like one more dependent child for us to raise. We'll care for her the same as we did for Jeremiah. She'll always have a home nearby, for we'll not let her become a public charge, one of those pitiful wretches at the Poor Farm."

Lizzie's heart swelled. "You're a good man, Brad Mathews, to accept the burden o' responsibility with no railin' nor complainin'."

He gave her a fond look, then reached across and took her tanned, work-toughened hand in his. "An' maybe, Lizzie Mathews, that's 'cause I'm married to a woman who's taught me well—"

chapter

15

ONE YEAR slipped by.

Then two.

Because Miss Abby needed constant supervision, the twins took turns attending class so someone could mind their stepmother and prevent her from wandering off during the day, or maybe even accidentally burning down the cabin when she was in one of her foggy spells.

Eventually, though she had remained strong many years after her mind failed, Miss Abby's physical health seemed to decline. Now, instead of "eating for two," she picked at her food, and Marissa or Molly would have to stand over her at mealtime and insist that she clean her plate.

Not only that, but she became increasingly susceptible to whatever illness might be plaguing the area, and Lizzie often sent glass-stoppered bottles of nostrums and herbal potions to the girls to dose Miss Abby in an attempt to keep up her strength and resistance.

On a chilly day in late October, during Molly's turn to mind her stepmother, Miss Abby began to cough. The young woman knew that in her mama's weakened condition even a mild case of the sniffles could lead to the grippe or perhaps even pneumonia, so she quickly threw on a cape and rushed to the woodpile for wood to feed the fire sputtering in the parlor hearth.

The western horizon was leaden. Storm clouds tumbled across the stern sky. A cold wind gusted, piercing her cloak and announcing that a drenching rain was imminent.

Stooping to select some firewood, Molly gathered an armload, then spotted a chunk of seasoned hickory as big around as her arm. This hefty piece would guarantee a fast, hot blaze and would leave plenty of embers with which to ignite more logs should a downpour drench the woodpile Lizzie's sons had cut and stacked for them.

Molly stepped up on a chunk of wood at the base of the pile, stood on tiptoe, and worked to extricate the piece of hickory.

Suddenly there came a rumble from within the pile. Too late, Molly realized that the hickory stob was a key block in the mound, loosing an avalanche of wood. Shifting and sliding, the pile thundered down upon her.

With a cry of alarm, she tried to spring out of the way but tripped and fell heavily, lengths of small cordwood clattering about her.

A piece of dislodged wood large enough to bank the fire in the hearth throughout the night tumbled down the pile. The length of cordwood seemed to flip lazily into the air, then with free-wheeling momentum, plunged toward the ground, landing on Molly's leg with a muffled thud that could not hide the sound of snapping bone.

The sudden agony left Molly feeling sick to her stomach, and she fought down retching sensations as cold sweat poured from her brow, leaving her unable to catch her breath.

"Mama! Help, Mama!" cried Molly as the searing ache ricocheted through her body. She could feel the flesh puff, grow fevered, and swell against the physical affront.

She tried to move but found that she could not. Unable to remove the logs that pinioned her to the ground, Molly was trapped, injured, and piteously alone. She knew it could be hours before anyone found her and came to her aid.

The chilly wind wrapped itself around her, enfolding Molly in an icy embrace that made her teeth chatter. Helplessly she shivered, and with each spasm that jarred her broken leg, fresh torment spiraled through her. A cold, light rain began to fall, quickly soaking the earth beneath the thatch of dried grasses.

It was Marissa, returning from school, who found Molly. Panting and straining, she hoisted the logs off her twin, then helped her to stand on her good leg while she propped herself under Molly's arm to act as a crutch.

"Where's Mama?" Marissa asked as the pair staggered into the cabin and Molly collapsed into a kitchen chair.

"She's not here? She wasn't here when you came home, Marissa?"

"No. I—I thought she was with you."

"She was in the parlor, amusin' herself with a checker game. I didn't have time to join her . . . but she seemed content to move the pieces about on her own. I only meant to leave her long enough to fetch wood. . . . I never dreamed I'd be trapped, that Mama'd be left unchaperoned—"

At that, Marissa uttered a harsh invective that Molly knew would have sent Lizzie Mathews scurrying for the lye soap. But at the moment Molly was too wracked with pain and worry to bother chastising her sister.

"I'll take a quick look around," Marissa decided. "It's for sure *you* can't."

"Hurry! Darkness is fallin'. I—I'll be all right 'til you return. But check the peg in the kitchen first and see if Mama took her wrap."

151

Marissa glanced into the adjacent area. "No. It's still here."

"Then surely she can't have gone far," Molly said, relieved.

Marissa gave a brittle laugh. "You'd be surprised! What thought would she give to needin' a warm wrap? Reality may be that winter's bearin' down on us fast, you goose, but in her pleasant fantasies, Mama may have convinced herself that it's a balmy day in May!"

"Please hurry, 'Rissa! It's threatening rain. If you don't find her soon, you'll have to summon Brad and the boys to help you look. Mama can't be out in a downpour with no warm garments to protect her from the elements . . . and the wild animals—" She closed her eyes, trying to shut out the vision of the terrors that stalked the dark woods.

A minute later the back door banged shut and Marissa was on her way.

Molly lowered her face to her hands and began to pray for God's merciful intervention. She prayed against the weather, the pain, the thought of never seeing their stepmother again.

Outside, Marissa bawled their stepmother's name again and again, then, as the girl trudged farther and farther from the cabin, her cries dissipated into the thin air. Finally her voice ceased carrying back to the cabin altogether.

Some time later, Molly could not be sure just how long, she heard lone steps on the path, and her heart grew heavy. Marissa was returning without Miss Abby.

Her pretty sister was sodden to the skin when she entered the house and shook water from her eyes, immodestly peeling off her wet dress and underwear to reveal an appealingly pert body.

"I couldn't find hide nor hair of Mama," she said as she tossed the soaked mess of clothing toward the corner of the kitchen where the copper washboiler lay and then reached for a towel. She wrapped it around her and paraded in front of the hearth, warming herself before she entered the bedroom to retrieve dry garments.

"What are we going to do?" Molly called after her.

"There's only one thing to do—," her sister began, "—get Brad." But Molly noticed that she made no move to leave their cozy cabin.

"Then . . . are you . . . that is, will you . . . go for him? I wish I could help, but—"

"I know!" Marissa replied shortly. "I can think on my own! I'm not as weak-minded as Ma."

"You don't have to be so mean—" Molly was trembling on the brink of tears, nerves frayed from anxiety and the ravages of the unceasing pain that throbbed in her leg until her foot now felt almost numb.

Marissa glanced at her. "I didn't mean to be," she offered by way of an apology. "I can't help it if I get disgusted over what goes on around here. It's not your fault any more than it is mine. We've got to do what we've got to do, though God knows I get sick and tired of it sometimes." She let out a long sigh. "If we consigned Ma to a loonybin where she could live with other crazy folks, they could drive one another insane and spare all us normal folks!"

Marissa looked up in time to see Molly wince. "Your leg . . . it's pretty bad. Do you need a doctor?"

"Yes, but not right now," Molly murmured. "Get help for Mama first. I can wait. For her sake . . . please hurry."

It was less than half an hour before Marissa returned with Brad and the boys, bearing coal-oil lanterns to light their way.

"Mama didn't come back while I was away, did she?" asked Marissa, panting for breath as she burst into the cabin.

"No."

Brad's face was strained. "Then, boys," he said to Lester and Thad, "we'd best start the search. We'll have to take our time and stay close together. In this storm it'll be easy to overlook her if we're not careful. 'Specially if she's tripped 'n' fallen."

"Should I go along to help?" Marissa asked, favoring Lester with a warm smile as she tossed her wavy hair over her shoulders.

Brad intercepted the look. "Stay here with your sister," he told Marissa. "She needs you more right now. How bad are you hurt, Molly? Your leg's broke, ain't it? Not just a sprain?"

"I—I heard the bone snap."

Brad shuddered then laid a gentle hand on her shoulder. "We'll get you to the doctor so's he can set it proper. But I can't be in two places at once—," he said helplessly.

"Mama needs you, Brad. I'll be all right. The pain . . . it's not so bad. Maybe if someone would bring me the Bible and set a lantern on the table, I could be almost comfortable while I'm waitin'."

Lester quickly moved to comply, and Molly gave him a grateful smile.

"Marissa," Molly said, "put some coffee on the stove. The men will need it to warm their bones when they return."

By now the men had stepped from the cabin, ducking into the sluicing downpour outside. And while Molly did her best, she could not get comfortable. She tried to read but she was unable to focus on the words, for her imagination conjured scenes that imprinted themselves on the pages as she idly turned them—Mama, frightened and alone; Mama, falling into the swollen waters of Salt Creek; Mama, tripping over a log; Mama, attacked by vicious wild animals—

The hours passed. Marissa had long since fallen asleep when Molly's eyes sagged shut at last, but rest evaded her, driven away by the gritty pain that emanated from her right leg.

It was almost dawn before Brad and the boys returned. Their haggard faces bore evidence of their sleepless night and the grim harvest they had reaped. In Brad's arms was a limp bundle.

"Mama!" cried Molly, beginning to weep.

"Miss Abby needs a doctor," said Brad quietly. "And so do you, Molly. But after the rain, Salt Creek is flooded bank to bank. There'll be no fordin' it for days, so we'll have to do the best we can. I'm takin' both o' you to Lizzie. She's doctored almost as many folks as the doc in town—"

Brad turned to Lester. "Bring the horse 'n' wagon, son. I'll carry Miss Abby out, then come back for Miss Molly. We'll cover 'em with a tarp from the shed in back o' the cabin to protect 'em from the weather."

Molly felt an agonizing stab when she tried to sit up. Her leg was swollen to twice its size, already discolored to a dark, mottled purple. She moaned softly when Brad entered the room, anticipating the pain in even his most gentle touch.

Gingerly, Brad lifted the hem of her dress enough to examine her leg and grimaced when he saw the area of the fracture. "Wish I could get you to the sawbones," he sighed, "but ain't no way, Molly-girl. I'm purely sorry. Looks like Lizzie'll have to set your leg herself. If we wait, the bone'll start knittin' itself, and then you'll never walk right again. She'll be gentle, but I'm thinkin' that even so, it'll be a torment. Still, the pain o' one night will be small compared to livin' out the rest o' your days with a limp."

Molly's face was ashen, but she nodded wordlessly.

"Put your arms around my neck to brace yourself," Brad instructed. "It's goin' to hurt to move you."

And it did. A helpless yipe escaped the injured girl's lips when Brad lifted her in his arms, jostling her to get a more secure grip. With Marissa looking on, he carried her to the wagon and laid her beside Miss Abby's still form as Lester waited to slide the piece of musty-smelling canvas into place.

"Is she goin' to live?" Molly asked, squinting to focus on Miss Abby's waxen features. Her stepmother's hair was wetly plastered to her scalp, making her look tiny and vulnerable.

Brad paused. "I don't rightly know. She's awful weak, and the rattle when she breathes sounds like she's already caught her death o' cold. I'd say her chances ain't good by human measurements, but with God, anythin' is possible."

"Has she said anything? Does Mama know anybody?"

"She's called for your pa a few times, but she ain't said anythin' else we could make out."

Molly sighed. "It's like she won't rest and know peace until she finds him."

Brad touched the faint pulse point in Miss Abby's neck. "That's apt to be this very night, Miss Molly," he said solemnly. "We'd better make haste . . . leastways, you ain't beyond help. Lizzie'll doctor you as best she can, and with time, maybe the day'll come when your leg's as good as new."

The trip to Lizzie's cabin was one of wrenching pain. Molly almost passed out from the white-hot throb in her leg when they transported her into the dwelling. But she rested on the horsehair sofa while Lester and Brad carried Miss Abby into Lizzie's bedroom, and waited while they piled her stepmother high with quilts and spooned herbal brews and broth into her, hoping the added warmth would work a miracle and bring her around.

"We'd best set that leg now, Molly," Lizzie decided as she left Abby in Harmony's care. "Brad, you 'n' the boys hold Molly down. I can't promise this won't be a livin' torment, darlin'," she told the girl, "but it's necessary if you're to walk normal again. I'd do 'bout anythin' to keep you from losin' your leg like my brother Rory."

All modesty was abandoned as Lester, Thad, and Brad pinioned Molly's arms and good leg while Marissa cowered in the adjoining room, covered her ears, and pinched her eyes tightly shut. Lizzie examined the damaged area of the fractured limb, shoving the plump twin's skirt up high on her thigh but leaving the protective rough black stocking in place on her other leg.

"I think I've got it figgered how it's got to go so's I can twist the limb and coax it back into place—," Lizzie said, then muttered under her breath, "—iffen it ain't already too swole to fit the way it ought." She handed Brad the lamp to hold with one hand while he secured Molly's arm with the other. "All right, brace yourselves! When I set this leg, like as not Molly's goin' to pass out. You can leave hold o' her then and hand me the bandages so's I can bind a splint on her leg to keep it straight and 'low the bone to knit, undisturbed."

"We're ready when you are, Liz," Brad quietly encouraged.

Lizzie paused a moment as if collecting her courage. "Y'all get ready. Now . . . one . . . two . . . three—" She leaned into the table, bracing with an apron-clad hip.

A shaft of blinding pain, white-hot, speared Molly's body and exploded behind her eyes as inner surfaces of the bone grated and shifted grittily, resisting before they acquiesced to the steady pressure of Lizzie's hands.

Crying out, begging them to stop, Molly bucked uselessly on the kitchen table where they'd laid her. She screamed as she arched against the almost unendurable pain. But she was no match for it. For them. The girl howled until her throat was raw, then yielded to the horror.

Then all was blackness, bringing blessed release from the relentless, rending pain as the bone sank into place. She lay as still on her pallet as Miss Abby did in Lizzie's bed, her breath so shallow that each exhalation seemed destined to be her last.

The faint gray light behind the drawn curtains had faded away, relinquishing to the darkness when an exhausted Lizzie tiptoed into the parlor where Molly lay.

"Molly? Are you awake?" There was an urgency in her tone that caused the girl to emerge from her stuporous sleep and crack her eyes open almost at once.

"What is it?"

"It's your mama. She's dyin', Molly, honey. I done my best, but there's nothin' more I can do. She was too far gone when they brought her in. Do you want to see her one last time?"

Choking on a sob, Molly nodded.

"Your leg's splinted good, so it won't do no damage if Brad 'n' the boys carry you in to her so's you can have a special good-bye, though I believe she's past knowin' ya."

Molly bore the pain as stoically as she had endured all else, thanking Brad and Lester for taking her to where her stepmother lay dying.

"Mama!" Molly whispered, clutching her hand, so thin and bony. She brought it to her own fevered cheek and let the hot tears fall on the pale, icy flesh. "I love you, Mama."

A moment later, Abby's fingers grew limp, and, with a long, soft sigh, one that sounded so very contented, she was gone.

"We'll attend to the buryin' this forenoon," Brad said quietly. "Lester can notify the neighbors who'll want to attend the committal services. As beloved as Miss Abby was by parents and students alike, there'll be a crowd gathered here today."

"I'll lay her out on the coolin' board," Lizzie said, "'n' wash her down and prepare her for viewin'."

"We've a burial box in the loft," Brad said. "Thad and Lester, I'll leave it to you to heft it down. Then collect some spades. After we have a bite o' breakfast, we'll open the grave while Ma 'n' Harmony attend to the needs of the dead."

"It's a pity that Mama can't be buried alongside Pa," Katie mourned when she arrived from the teacherage.

"That can't be helped," Lizzie said, putting her arm around the girl, then felt a stab of sympathy for the Wheelers, who were no longer free to visit the gravesites of their ma and pa now that unfriendly owners held the deed to the land. "Miss Abby will repose among friends—Jeremiah . . . Maylon . . . 'n' Harmon."

chapter
16

THE GOLDEN weeks of autumn slipped by, and Molly's season of healing progressed as winter winds blew wild and free.

Following Miss Abby's passing, Alton's twins lived alone in the house that had once belonged to Fanny and Will Preston, even though the situation vexed Lizzie's sense of propriety. And with men who were anything but gentlemen residing in the community, it was not only unseemly but downright dangerous! Still, Lizzie was somewhat mollified when she heard rumors that the two scoundrels actually spent little time at the former Wheeler farm, so busy were they enjoying high times and creating a ruckus at the various places of iniquity to be found in the county seat town to the north.

"The twins *are* nearby, Liz, livin' in the shadow of your influence. Surely that'll stand 'em in good stead," Brad said one day when for the umpteenth time, Lizzie broached the subject of the Wheeler girls' safety and training.

"Well, I just can't help worryin' about 'em—two comely young women, with no man to offer his protection."

Brad gave her a studied look. "From what I've heard tell, the men who swindled Miss Abby out o' their farm tend to keep to themselves 'n' their own kind. They don't neighbor with anyone in the community. There's more'n a good chance they're even unaware that Molly and Marissa ain't livin' under the protection of our roof come evenin'."

"An' we can be thankful for *that*," Lizzie murmured. "But Molly confided in me how outraged she was one day last week when those two passed by on their way home from town, and Marissa waved to 'em from the woodpile in the side yard."

Brad was shaken. "God help us! That's all the encouragement those rapscallions would need to draw improper conclusions."

"My worries, exactly."

"Maybe we ought to consider fellin' some more trees, haulin' the logs to a sawyer, and tackin' another addition onto this cabin that's already sprawlin' every which way—"

Their conversation was cut short by Lemont Gartner's unexpected arrival. They watched as a serious-faced Lemont stamped the snow from his boots and entered Lizzie's warm kitchen, where bread dough was rising on a sideboard.

"'Mornin', Lem. Have a seat, 'n' I'll get you some coffee," Lizzie said in a pleasant voice.

To her surprise, the elderly man remained standing and gave her such an assessing stare that her skin crawled.

He licked his lips. "I'd 'a' thought you were more your mama's daughter than you're now rumored to be."

Lizzie was stunned. "Exactly what's that supposed to mean?" she asked, helpless to control her voice which rose a little in consternation.

Lemont stood his ground and stared back. "All these years I've thought you were a forgivin' woman, Elizabeth Preston Mathews."

Lizzie, feeling unfairly attacked, felt her limbs grow weak. Being accused of something she couldn't fathom, by a family friend who should have known the kind of person she was,

was almost more than she could bear, and a flood of tears was scarcely more than a blink away.

"I try, Lemont Gartner," she said in a choked tone. "I have my faults, failin's, and weaknesses, same as anyone else, but I've always tried. An' that's a heap more'n some folks!"

The old man wiped frost from his spectacles with a bright red handkerchief. "Granted you forgive me, 'n' some others, too. So why do you refuse to forgive your own brother?"

The room seemed to spin around Lizzie. "Refuse . . . to forgive Rory? What in the name of heaven are you talkin' about, Lemont? If somehow you think you're funnin' me, this ain't amusin'! Exactly what are you drivin' at?"

"You mean you don't . . . know?"

"Know? Know what?!" Lizzie cried.

Convinced of her innocence, Lemont was chagrined and immediately regretted blustering into her kitchen with his charges.

"What's taken place, Lem, that's gotten you so riled up?" Brad asked, stepping in to mediate.

"When I was in Effingham, I saw Lizzie's brother."

Lizzie leaped from the chair where she'd collapsed and clasped Lemont's arm. "You saw Rory? Are you sure? It wasn't hearsay? Someone's idea of a joke?"

"It's hardly amusin', Miss Lizzie. Rory's back in town. I saw him with my own eyes . . . talked to him as I'm speakin' to you now."

"Oh . . . my—," Lizzie stammered, dropping back into her chair as if her legs could no longer be trusted to support her.

"He was askin' 'bout you, Miss Lizzie, inquirin' of folks he chanced to meet in the Gen'ral Store and 'round the liv'ry. When I approached Rory, he recognized me right off, 'n' I told him news of the fam'ly."

"How . . . how is he? How has my brother fared?"

Lemont shrugged. "Very well, I'd say, judgin' by appearances."

"Then he's well?"

"Yes, though he's almost sick with grievin'. It's sorely tried his heart, Miss Lizzie, this hardness he's found in yours—"

"But that's not true!" she protested. "Do tell me what you're talkin' about!"

"Mind you I'm only reportin' the situation, but Rory feels you ain't willin' to forgive 'im. I 'lowed as how he was likely wrong. But beats me if I knew what to say when he asked why you'd ignored his letter beggin' your forgiveness."

"I—I didn't ignore it, Lem! If I'd ever received such a letter, 'twould have purely busted my heart with joy! An I'd have answered it! I swear I would've . . . 'n' made a special trip to town to post my answer, too!"

"That's true, Lem," Brad interjected. "Rory's return has been a constant prayer on Lizzie's lips these long years."

"I told Rory he oughta travel back out to his old community to pay a visit, but he claims he ain't got the will to confront you, Lizzie, for fear of how he'd be received. He's hurt deep 'n' bitter disappointed that his letter went unanswered. Claims he wrote to you from Colorady, but when you never wrote back, he didn't try to contact you again."

"Well, I never got any letter, and it seems plain that he never accepted deliv'ry of mine, neither. O' course they was sent in care o' Gen'ral Deliv'ry, where he could've received 'em only if he happened to be in the right city at the right time."

Lemont shook his head over the ironies. "I'm sorry for misjudgin' you, Lizzie. I should've knowed better."

She nodded brusquely, still stinging from her neighbor's rebuke. Right now, however, she was more interested in learning every detail of her brother's welfare. "An' how is Rory . . . really?"

"He's a credit to your folks, Lizzie Mathews, a true gent— as upright a man as you'd ever hope to meet."

Lizzie closed her eyes, hugging herself with joy. "Thank God! Oh, praise God!"

"He's not the man who ran away and sold the farm without your knowledge, Miss Lizzie. Since that sad departure, he's returned to the way of his raisin'. I'd say he's a brother to do you proud."

"I must go to him at once! Where is he?"

"At the Benwood Hotel."

"Get ready, darlin', 'n' we'll leave right away," Brad said, grinning. "Perhaps Lemont will be good enough to finish tendin' to the bread that's almost ready to bake."

He gave a nod of assent. "I should warn you in advance . . . Rory's not alone. H—he's got his fam'ly with him—his wife, her name is Sylvia . . . refined 'n' eddicated . . . 'n' a little girl, sweet and purty as you please."

Lizzie could take no more. She burst into sobs and flung herself into Brad's arms. "This'll be the best Thanksgiving ever, what with Rory and his fam'ly givin' thanks and eatin' hearty 'round our table."

Brad had hitched up the team and was ready to go by the time Lizzie propped a note against the kerosene lamp in the center of the table and rushed from the cabin, calling her thanks to Lemont over her shoulder, and closing the door securely behind her.

No sooner had Brad helped Lizzie into the wagon than he took his place, clucked to the horses, and set out at a brisk trot.

Taking a direct route, they pulled up before the Benwood

Hotel only two hours later. Lizzie patted her hair into place, shook the wrinkles from her dress, and prepared to alight.

The first fluffy snowflakes had begun falling when Brad steered Lizzie across the brick street and into the hotel lobby.

"May I help you?" asked the same clerk who had handled their business on their honeymoon.

"We'd like to see a Mister and Missus Rory Preston," Brad spoke up. "We understand they're stayin' here."

"Right you are," he said and provided the room number. "If they're not in their quarters, we'll be glad to take a message, or you can wait in the lobby."

The idea of waiting, when her patience had been worn thinner than an old piece of lye soap already, was almost more than Lizzie could bear. "Come on!" She grabbed Brad's arm and headed down the corridor.

"This's it." He squinted at the number affixed to the door. "Are you ready?"

Lizzie felt herself grow pale and clung to Brad's arm, not sure she wouldn't swoon as he rapped on the door.

"One moment please," came a woman's pleasant voice.

The door opened a crack. The woman regarded the pair in confusion. Lizzie stared back, stunned. The woman was magnificent—pretty, sweet-faced, and with a congenial expression on her face.

"May I help you?"

"I'm Lizzie . . . 'n' I'm here to see my brother, Rory."

"Lizzie!" Sylvia repeated, her voice tremulous. "I've heard so very much about you. Do come in!" She took Lizzie's hand and led her into the room.

Rory was nowhere in sight. A small child slept on a cot nearby.

"Who was at the door, darlin'?"

For the first time in years, Lizzie heard Rory's voice, and her heart melted at the sound.

Sylvia squeezed Lizzie's hand, bidding her be silent, and winked. "We've callers, dear. Come and make them welcome."

When he entered the room, Rory stared in disbelief, speechless. Then came a whoop of joy, and he opened his arms to Lizzie. They flew into each other's embrace, laughing, crying, both talking at once.

"Rory," Lizzie said, drawing Brad into the circle. "I'd like you to meet my husband, Brad Mathews."

"I'm afraid we've already met," Rory said with a wry grin, "under very dif'rent circumstances."

"You see how completely your sister has forgiven you?" Brad teased. "She's put from mind all o' your past misdeeds."

"Well, I've been tellin' Sylvia 'bout her for years . . . how I never thought she'd be one to hold a grudge . . . though it did look that way for a while—"

Sylvia slipped her arm through Rory's. "You were right in the first place," she said. "Your sister is everything you said she'd be."

Rory regarded Lizzie fondly. "And she . . . and Mama . . . serve as fine examples for the little one who bears their names. Come see our Fanchon Elizabeth . . . we call her Fanny Beth!"

"Oh, Rory—," Lizzie spoke in a wondering tone. "I never thought a young'un would ever be named for *me!* This is like a dream. . . ." She looked at the angelic child who was sleeping with one chubby fist tucked under a rosy cheek.

"Not a dream . . . a *miracle!*"

"So what're you goin' to do now, Rory?" Lizzie asked when she could collect her wits and they had been seated in the small sitting area.

He shrugged. "I haven't made up my mind yet. Over the years I worked in the gold mines in Colorado, the lumber camps in Oregon, and held a few itinerant jobs in between. Invested some money . . . did right well in the mines, too . . . and better in timberin' . . . enough to stake me to a business of my own when I figure out what I want to do. Loggin's kind of gotten into my blood, but I'm gettin' older, and workin' in the woods—'specially hilly terrain—is hard for a man with only one good leg." He gazed out through the window, focusing on nothing in particular. "I've been thinkin' of financin' a sawmill, Lizzie, and hirin' others to help me with the work."

Lizzie and Brad exchanged shocked glances, then burst into a peal of delighted laughter.

"We could sure use a sawmill out in our neck o' the woods, Rory," Brad spoke up. "It's like an answer to prayer!"

"An' Salt Creek's surrounded by good hardwood timber," Lizzie pointed out.

"The area's boomin', Rory," Brad added. "There'll be a need for sawed lumber for construction."

"I guess what we're tryin' to say," Lizzie said softly, "is that we want . . . we're beggin' . . . you 'n' your family to stay."

"I–I'd like to—" Rory gave Sylvia a searching look.

She smiled and lowered her eyes in acceptance. "A long time ago I vowed that 'whither thou goest, I will go.'"

"Then where you're both goin' is to our farm . . . 'n' don't give me no neverminds about it!" Lizzie insisted. "Now that we've found one 'nother, I ain't lettin' you out o' my sight, Rory Preston!"

"That's the Lizzie I remember," he said, laughing. "Always orderin' me about! Fussin' and cluckin' over me like a feisty bantam hen with a wayward chick."

"Some things never change, Rory," Brad said, rising stiffly

from the chair. "Now if Miss Sylvia can attend to packin' the valises, I'll lend a hand with your baggage, and we can have you home by nightfall."

"Home—," Rory said, dazed.

"Home is where the heart is," Sylvia sighed, and reached for the baby who was stirring to wakefulness. She hugged Fanny Beth tightly. "We're goin' home, darlin' girl ... home!"

chapter
17

WHEN BRAD halted the wagon in the side yard, all the young'uns—his and Lizzie's—spilled out of the cabin, calling their greetings, eager to see the newcomers.

Rory hopped lightly from the wagon, favoring his bad leg. "Where are you goin' to put us, Lizzie?" he asked, noting the expanded family. "You hauled us here, but it appears you'll be hard-pressed to find space for us."

"We're goin' to hang you from hooks in the rafters, 'n' take you down at mealtime," she bantered, then grew serious. "Aw, Rory, you know what Mama used to say: 'There's always room for one more!'"

"You're a lot like Ma," Rory decided, giving her an appraising look.

"That's sweet of you to say. C'mon in," Lizzie said, leading the way. "The cabin's a sight . . . we left in such a hurry. But it's home to us . . . 'n' to you, too, for as long as you're wantin' to stay."

"It's lovely, really lovely, Lizzie," Sylvia said, taking in the room at a glance, observing the crisp curtains and warm colors, a room that bore Lizzie's loving touch. "You've so many nice things."

"When you 'n' Rory set up housekeepin', I'll pass on some

of Mama's treasures for you to enjoy and someday pass down to Fanny Beth. Mama'd like that."

"My, but it's goin' to be good to be here with you, Sis. We've much to catch up on. We'll hate to leave in a few days," Rory admitted.

"You just got here!" protested Brad, coming in from stabling the horses. "Let's hear no talk of leavin'!"

"We can't be puttin' your family out on our account."

"Where are you plannin' on going?" Lizzie asked. "Not far away, I hope."

"Sylvia and I haven't talked about it. But since I've put back money, we'd like to buy a place of our own. It's a matter of findin' a suitable tract with a cabin already constructed, I'd hope."

"But I'm afraid you won't be close enough for visitin', Rory."

"Yes he will, darlin'," Brad said, "if he buys back the land where he was born. I'm willin' to sell him back the Preston place."

"Oh, you dear man! What do you think, Rory?" Lizzie asked, turning to her brother after bestowing a radiant smile on Brad.

"It—it would be a dream come true. How many times I've rued sellin' Pa's land."

"And, how many times I've thanked the good Lord you *did,* Rory Preston," Brad countered, "or I'd have never come to know the wonderful woman I now claim for my wife."

"It was meant to be, Rory," Lizzie said, blushing. "You know how the Lord is . . . takin' somethin' awful 'n' makin' it over into somethin' purely wonderful! We had to know sadness and loss so's we could better appreciate our blessin's."

"I can't thank both of you enough!" Rory was nearly

speechless for the second time that day. "It will be so good to be home . . . so good."

To Lizzie's surprise, there was a hint of moisture in her brother's eyes. Lemont was right. This was not the same callous young man who had left her cabin that day so long ago.

Suddenly Lizzie and Brad looked at each other in a quick, stark stare, their faces flushing when they realized exactly what they'd done. But Rory and Sylvia didn't notice, or if they did, may have reasoned that the ruddiness of their hosts' complexions was due to the heat rushing from the roaring fire on the hearth.

Later, Lizzie and Brad prepared for bed in silence, then drew the quilts up snug. They lay still, their thoughts racing.

It was Lizzie who broke the silence at last. "Brad, what're we going to do 'bout Rory 'n' Sylvia? They can't move into my folks' place with Molly and Marissa there!"

He sighed. "I know—"

"Usually it's me who's the impetuous one, and you that's given to thinkin' long and hard before speakin'."

"I know," he said again. "It just seemed the right thing to do. Besides, I saw it as a way to give happiness to you 'n' Rory, too."

"—while bringin' misery and rejection to the Wheeler girls. It's the same as turnin' 'em out, Brad, offerin' Rory the farm like you did."

"But what's done is done, Liz," he said miserably.

"Not that I can really say I'm sorry you done it," she said soothingly. "In the excitement o' Rory's homecomin', the presence of the Wheeler girls at the ol' homeplace slipped my mind, too. You saw how happy he was, Brad. We just can't go back on the offer now."

He thought on. "Maybe we could put Molly and Marissa

up for a while so's Rory 'n' his fam'ly could have their home soon. After what I promised Rory, Liz, that's what we *have* to do. Don't see no way 'round it."

"'Pears to be the only way."

"Then we'll speak to the girls on Thanksgivin'." With the decision made, Brad felt only a little relief.

"I'm of a mind that someone oughtta speak to Molly and Marissa before then so's they can get used to the idea," Lizzie mused. "I'll walk over first thing in the mornin' 'n' speak to 'em, afore you collect 'em for school—"

"School!" Brad exclaimed. "Why didn't we think of it? They can live at the teacherage with our Linda, and their sister, Katie Wheeler!"

"Why, I declare, you're right! But I don't want Alton's girls feelin' like burdens or charity cases. So I sincerely hope they'll be acceptin' of the arrangements—"

"They have to. There's nowhere else for 'em to go."

"Nowhere but the County Poor Farm."

"*Never!*" they whispered in unison.

Lizzie arose early the next morning, eager to make the trip to her ma and pa's old place in order to explain the change in plans to Molly and Marissa Wheeler as gently and as soon as possible.

"Lizzie, is somethin' the matter?" Molly asked with concern.

"This is a most unusual time to come callin'," Marissa added.

"As a matter of fact," Lizzie said, removing her scarf and loosening her cloak, "I do have something I wish to discuss with you girls."

"Well, you might as well have a seat."

Lizzie decided to get right to the heart of the matter.

"Yesterday, my brother, Rory Preston, returned to the area with his new fam'ly. Maybe you remember him. . . ."

The girls looked at each other and nodded. "We'll be lookin' forward to makin' their acquaintance on Thanksgiving Day—" Molly hesitated. "That is, if you still want us . . . providin' there's room."

"Of course we do!" Lizzie insisted. "Of course there is!"

"Will your brother be stayin' . . . long?" Marissa asked, suddenly suspicious.

Lizzie heaved a sigh. "That's the problem I've come to speak to you about, girls," she went on quickly. "Rory and his fam'ly will be movin' here . . . into this house."

There was not a sound to be heard in the cabin except for the thunderous tick-tock of the wall clock.

"Oh . . . my!" Molly murmured.

Marissa sat stiffly erect, her back rigid, her face a stony mask. "And what about *us?*"

"Why, you can reside at the teacherage with your sister Katie 'n' Linda Mathews," Lizzie tried to explain. "'Twill be fun . . . you'll see."

"Oh," Molly said in a small voice.

Marissa said nothing.

Like the still before a storm, Molly thought. Marissa seemed too calm, and she feared that her sister would fly into a fit of temper.

"Oh, girls . . . I'm so sorry," Lizzie apologized. "I know what a blow this must be, how you must be feelin'. But don't look so glum. It'll work out somehow, 'n' it's the only solution we have. Like my mama used to say, 'When one door closes, the Lord opens a window somewhere else.' Maybe this is an opportunity for all o' us."

"Perhaps," Molly said before tense silence reigned once more.

"Please say somethin'!" Lizzie cried. "Don't just stand there like lil' whipped pups. I hate doin' this to you, girls, more'n you'll ever know."

"We'll be packed and ready to move out any time you say," was Molly's careful reply. "Don't worry over us."

Marissa said nary a word.

Lizzie's heart ached when she got ready to depart for home and saw Molly, with her broken leg, limping about on the crutch Brad had fashioned out of a hickory sapling to bear her weight until the limb was fully healed.

"Hurry, Marissa," Molly urged after Lizzie departed, "or we'll be late to school."

Marissa moved to the window and stood looking out. Molly stumped to her side, leaned on the crude crutch, and watched, too, until Lizzie was a speck on the trail. At the bend in the road she disappeared altogether.

Resigned, Molly turned away.

Marissa did, too, her chin granite hard, her eyes sparking like lightning across a stormy summer sky. Then something snapped within her. Unable to contain her rage at the unfairness of Lizzie's proposal, she screamed an oath. Then another.

Caught in the grip of her fury, she knocked a vase from a table and watched as it shattered, giving direction to her anger.

"'Rissa, tomorrow's Thanksgiving," Molly reminded her. "At least we can be thankful we'll have a roof over our heads—" She paused. "I wonder how soon they'll be wantin' us to move out?"

"Immediately, you can be sure."

"And it's goin' to take a while to pack our belongin's," Molly said in dismay, her gaze sweeping the crowded room.

"So it will," Marissa agreed, now strangely calm and

efficient. "Then we'd best get to work. Maybe . . . I should stay here and start packin', Molly. There's no sense in my goin' to school today when there's so much to do here."

"Then I'll stay and help."

"No, you go on to school. Crippled up as you are, you tire so easily, and it'd be too awkward for you to help with the packin'. Get ready, so you're waitin' when Brad comes by with the wagon."

"You're right," Molly agreed.

"I reckon I am," Marissa said and escaped to the kitchen before her sister could see the spark in her eyes and the angry set to her lips and consider what plans might be afoot.

A few minutes later Marissa emerged with Molly's lunch, packed in a tin lard pail. Then she fetched her sister's worn winter wrap and helped her into it, snugging it around her shoulders, and giving her a little pat as she did so.

"Have a good day, Molly."

"Good-bye, Marissa," Molly called out as she opened the door.

"Good-bye," Marissa replied softly. "Goodbye 'n' good luck," she added under her breath.

When the cabin door slammed shut, it was as final as the closing of a book.

Marissa stood at the window and watched Molly leave. Idly she wondered if she would ever see her twin sister again. Well, little matter. With so much to accomplish, there was no time for sentimentality.

Marissa's feet flew across the floor as she scurried about the rooms, opened a large trunk, and tucked in the possessions that Molly would need when she took up residence at the teacherage. She closed the lid and turned the lock.

Then she fetched crates from the storage sheds and packed the rest of their belongings into the slatted boxes. Stacking them in the corner, she slapped the dust from her hands with finality. That was that. The Mathewses could do with the crates as they pleased. It was no longer a concern of hers now, nor would it ever be again.

Hastily Marissa remade the bed. Molly might need to spend another night or two here, she reasoned.

Once more she inspected the cabin. What possessions remained, aside from the furniture that had been inherited from Brad and Fanny Preston's household, would surely revert to the care of Rory and his wife. Any other items Molly might need could be hastily gathered up at the last minute. But for all intents and purposes, the packing was complete.

It was noon when Marissa bathed quickly, changed into her best frock, put another good dress into a carpetbag along with her hairbrush, mirror, and a few mementos, and then fixed her hair in as fetching a style as she'd ever created.

Struggling with some heavy logs, she rolled them onto the fire, taking care not to soil her dress or dirty her hands. The fire would keep the cabin warm, and the coals should hold until Molly's return, when her sister could stoke the embers anew with the firewood Marissa had hauled in and neatly stacked nearby.

"There!" she said softly, and the whisper seemed to echo through the lonely cabin. "There—" For a moment Marissa suffered a pang of nostalgia, but she forced the troublesome thoughts away and gaily considered a future that was within reach and beyond the intrusion of others.

Marissa reached for the latch, plucked up her carpetbag, then bent to blow out the coal oil lamp. She stepped outdoors, closing the door behind her for the last time. Nervously, she glanced in all directions before she rushed down the frozen trail.

When Marissa neared the creek, she looked up and down

the stream in hopes of spying a log fallen across the breadth that she might cross. The dull brown water, in which dead leaves floated lazily, was much too icy. If she took off her shoes and stockings and waded across, she'd catch her death!

She was still studying the problem when a carriage clattered down the slope leading to the banks of the Salt Creek. Marissa's heart faltered. She dodged into a thicket, cowering low, her green eyes wide and wary as she watched for the passersby.

A moment later, as the conveyance drew into sight, she realized that the passengers were strangers to her. Since they would not care one whit whether she stayed here or departed the area, she stepped from her hiding place, shaking the brambles from her clothing. Considering that they might give her a ride to spare her the effort of walking all the way to Effingham, she waggled her fingers at the driver of the aging carriage.

But as she stepped into the light, she saw a pair of riders on horseback, making directly for her. It was the two high-living gents who had snookered Miss Abby out of the family farm! To her horror, the carriage rolled on down the road, and she was left with the two ruffians.

The tall one drew in on the reins.

The short one gave Marissa an appraising look.

"What're you doin' out here all by your lonesome, lil' lady?" asked the taller one, casting her a rakish smile.

Marissa dared to grin in reply. "Hopin' that some kind folks will take pity on me and offer me a ride to Effingham."

"Why, we'll be honored, if you're agreeable," replied the shorter, stouter fellow.

"Oh, I'm an agreeable one!" Marissa promised, and her words provoked a bawdy laugh.

"And why might you be going to Effingham, miss?"

"To seek my fortune."

"As are we," came a jovial admission. "We've a powerful thirst, a desire to woo purty ladies, and an urge to know some excitement."

Marissa sighed, then fluttered her eyes coquettishly, pouting prettily. She would not allow herself to consider the reaction of her sisters or Lizzie Mathews, let alone Pa Wheeler, if he'd lived to see her behaving thus. But *it couldn't be helped,* she thought. She simply had to get away!

"Why, with two swains as handsome as you, no doubt the ladies will be standin' in line for your attentions, livin' in hope of a smile." She dabbed at the corner of her eye with her handkerchief. "My little heart breaks when I know that I stand no chance a'tall—"

The two men gave one another yet another unbelieving look.

"Why, you're a beauty to make the ladies of the town hang their heads in shame, what with your fair features and fine figger!" one declared.

His partner nodded emphatically. "Were it not that we're partners 'n' friends, we'd be duelin' for the favor o' your comp'ny."

"How you do run on!" Marissa trilled. "Such teasin' could break a poor country girl's heart!"

"No doubt you've broken many hearts a'ready!" came the accusation.

"Never!"

"Then we'll wager you *will*, but it won't be one o' our'n!" And with that declaration, they threw back their heads and let out a loud guffaw.

For Marissa, the ride to Effingham, in the company of the two men, progressed well beyond her expectations. As they neared town, she already knew that she'd not be ungallantly discharged upon their arrival, for the pair had asked her to be their Lady Luck in the local gambling establishment.

Their destination was the livery and straightaway the saloon. Marissa quaked when she thought of what Pa would do if he knew she was about to sashay into a saloon. Or . . . Lizzie!

But she pushed those nettlesome thoughts from mind just as she dismissed everything else from the past that threatened to spoil the vision of the exciting, new life that awaited just beyond the swinging doors.

chapter
18

DUSK WAS draping the hills when Molly stumped home from school, the tip of her hickory crutch worn raggedy from continued impact against the frozen ground.

She opened the door and let herself in, surprised that Marissa hadn't come out to greet her and speak a word with Brad before he continued on home.

Embers in the hearth glowed low. There was a pile of kindling and a few logs stacked beside the fire as if Marissa had been interrupted just as she was about to stoke the flames.

"Marissa?" Molly called. There was only a ringing silence. "Sis!"

The stillness was unnerving. Nameless fear tingled down her spine. Exhausted, she leaned on her crutch, with not an inkling of where to search first. Brad had already disappeared, and she felt alone and helpless. Something terrible must have happened during her absence!

Then she saw the note.

She rushed into the kitchen as fast as she was able and over to the table, falling into a chair under the impact of the stunning news neatly penned on the scrap of paper.

Marissa was gone. Gone for good!

No! No! She couldn't let her go through with it! Who

knew what dangers awaited such an innocent, thought Molly, with more maturity than her years should have allowed. She had to save her sister . . . if only from herself!

Molly hobbled onto the large stone that served as the stoop of Lizzie Mathews's cabin, and, winded, leaned against the door, scarcely able to lift her hand and knock.

"Heavens, Molly! What's wrong? Brad, come quick!" Lizzie cried when she found the exhausted girl at her doorstep.

In a moment he was at her side. "What's happened, Miss Molly?"

"Marissa . . . she's gone . . . run away!" Molly managed.

"Run away?"

"Set out to make her own way in the world. Please . . . you've got to help me find her!"

Brad's expression sobered as did Rory's when he heard the news.

"We'll go after her 'n' bring her back," Brad promised.

Rory was quick to agree. "The world I walked through for a time is no place for a young girl on her own. Count me in."

Lester's ashen face was grim. "Me, too, Pa. I can't let Marissa ruin her life 'n' run outa mine so's I risk never seein' her again. I've always cared about her . . . too much . . . to let that happen—"

All eyes fell on the boy, suddenly seeing what had gone unnoticed by all of them. He loved Marissa! Why hadn't they realized it before? worried Lizzie.

Brad, too, felt a pang of guilt. Oh, he had detected the young girl's flirtatious manner but had suspected it was the result of losing her mother at such an early age and not having a strong woman's loving influence. Miss Abby had been failing mentally for so many years that she had not been able to curb the feisty twin's nature and lead her gently into young womanhood. But he had not given much thought to Lester's feelings for Marissa.

Now the truth of the boy's dilemma touched him. Man-to-man, he could not deny his son the opportunity to rescue the woman he loved. "Then we'll welcome your aid," Brad said now. "An' Godspeed to us all. Let's pray no misfortune finds Miss Marissa before *we* do."

"What about me, Pa?" Thad asked, sensing the excitement and wanting to be part of it.

Brad shook his head. "You're needed at home, boy. We don't know how long we'll have to be away, nor what we'll find when we get there. You must be here to take care of Mama 'n' Aunt Sylvia 'n' the girls."

Lizzie had quickly prepared a hamper of food for them to take along. She hefted it toward Brad, who had dressed against the bitterly cold night. "God be with you." She touched his cheek with the back of her hand. "An' we'll be prayin' you get home in time for our Thanksgivin' meal . . . with the added blessin' of seein' Marissa safe 'n' sound."

The next morning dawned blustery and cold. Stinging pellets of snow were borne on icy blasts of wind.

"It's an awful day," grunted Lemont Gartner, who had been persuaded to stay in out of the cold and nurse a lingering cough.

"We'll consider it a beautiful one if the menfolk bring Marissa home," Lizzie declared.

"In this storm, they surely won't be home for hours . . . maybe not even for days," sighed Sylvia with uncharacteristic pessimism.

"I–I'm scared," Molly admitted.

Lizzie patted her shoulder. "A body feels helpless when

there's nothin' to do 'cept hope 'n' pray. Poor Lester. To think I'd overlooked how taken he was with Marissa. How he must be feelin'. . . ."

Their Thanksgiving meal, while bountiful, was bleak. Lemont had long since departed for home, and night had fallen when Molly lay down to rest and promptly fell asleep.

Sylvia rocked Fanny Beth by the fire.

Thad whittled a toy to present to Rory's little one when she awoke.

Lizzie almost wore out the rag rug by the window, crossing the room to peer out in hopes of catching a flicker of light moving along the trail. But fatigued by the long day's activities, she, too, fell asleep on the horsehair sofa.

The fire was waning when she was awakened by sounds echoing in the brittle night air. She hefted a log onto the embers, then rushed to the window. The men were home! In the pale light of dawn she could see that Marissa was not with them—

She rushed to meet them, thankful that Molly was still sleeping.

"Marissa . . . she's—" The word caught in Lizzie's throat.

Brad was grim-faced. "Gone. We just missed her. From what we heard tell around town, she boarded a train bound for Chicago 'bout an hour or two 'fore we got into Effingham."

He handed the reins to a stricken Lester, who looked as if he were on the brink of tears.

Stiffly Rory alit from the conveyance. "I'm sorry, Liz. We were just too late to stop her."

"This's awful!" Lizzie cried. "We've been prayin' for her safety. I felt sure the Lord would hear our pleas—"

"All we can do is trust in His Word that all things work for good for those who love Him, darlin'," Brad gently reminded her.

"How's Lester takin' it?"

"He's plumb shook," Brad murmured. "Reckon the boy must've been sweet on her for months . . . for years . . . with none o' us any the wiser. Likely he was content to admire her beauty 'n' high spirits from afar."

Lizzie shook her head in wonder. "I'd a never thought to pair my Lester with a gal like Marissa. Molly, maybe, but never Marissa. That girl's as rebellious as Molly is dependable 'n' sweet-natured 'n' good."

"Well, we'll have to mind our mouths not to speak ill of Marissa, if only out of consideration for Lester. This is hard enough on him as 'tis. He knows what she's done is dead wrong, but love can somehow overlook a lot that most folks ain't so quick to forgive."

"Got anything to eat, Sis?" Rory asked. "We're famished, even though we feel hollow with dread over what's become of Miss Marissa."

"I'll have vittles on quick as a wink, 'n' then you can rest your bones abed, for you all must be powerful tired."

Lizzie ushered them into the house and plied them with hot coffee and flapjacks. When they'd eaten their fill, they drifted off to their beds, leaving only Lizzie, Brad, Rory, and Sylvia at the table. Lester, his face haunted, had already put on wraps and gone to the barn, offering to do the morning chores.

"What really happened, Brad?" Lizzie asked. "You just sketched in the barest details. I keep wonderin' if there's more you didn't tell out o' respect for Lester's feelin's."

Brad sighed. "There's more, all right, a story as sordid as they get. Marissa hitched a ride to town with those gents who used to own the Wheeler farm. She linked up with 'em but only long enough for a barroom fight to break out yesterday afternoon."

"Oh, heavens no—"

"There was some ugliness durin' a poker game," Brad went on. "Accusations resultin' in bloodshed. The sheriff was called out. Seems one o' the men who had interest in Alton's farm is dead—shot durin' the argument."

Lizzie and Sylvia grew pale. "This is worse than I'd imagined," Lizzie whispered. "But go on . . . tell us everythin' 'fore Lester returns."

"My guess is he'll be gone a while, grievin' out in the barn by his lonesome. But anyways, the other feller, with Marissa in his comp'ny, high-tailed it north on the next Illinois Central train headin' for Chicago. But that was only after sellin' off the ol' Wheeler spread. It was bought up by a feller who promptly turned 'round 'n' lost it in a poker game!" Lizzie's eyes had grown wide as the story unfolded.

"The winner hadn't any use for the plot o' ground, so's he was glad to get shed o' it by sellin' it off to a willin' buyer. One small blessin' in this whole sorry situation is that it's good riddance to that outfit. The community's better off without their likes among us," Brad concluded.

"What will become o' the Wheeler farm now?"

"The new owner has plans for it," Brad said mysteriously.

"If we're goin' to have new neighbors, I pray to God they'll be a decent sort," said Lizzie fervently, "but allowin' as how they were in a saloon buyin' up properties, I ain't holdin' out much hope for that."

"I laid eyes on the feller as he tendered his jack and took receipt of the deed, an' I was impressed with him. Lester seemed to be, too. Fact is, he's salt o' the earth to my way o' thinkin'. But reckon you'll have to decide for yourself, Liz."

"How soon are they plannin' to move in, so's we can go

callin' to welcome them to the community?" she wanted to know.

Somehow Brad managed to contain the grin that threatened to escape, and settled for a quick wink in Rory's direction. "The feller's sittin' next to you, darlin'. Your brother bought the Wheeler farm!"

Lizzie turned and stared, dumbfounded, at a grinning Rory who waved the deed before her eyes.

"*You*, Rory? But why? You already have a farm. You bought Ma 'n' Pa's place back from Brad."

"I'm a timberin' man, Sis," Rory Preston reminded her. "I need trees to be logged to saw into lumber. And there's a fine stand of timber on the Wheeler place. Plus, there's a comfortable cabin . . . big enough for a family. I'll need a place like that to offer my foreman if I expect him to move all the way to Illinois from the Pacific Northwest!"

"This is all movin' so fast, I'm right dizzy," Lizzie complained, putting her hand to her head. "Y'all talk 'n' I'll listen. But tell me all about it, 'n' don't leave out a *thing*."

Rory spoke on about his plans to construct a sawmill, hire a crew, and bring Seth Wyatt, Sylvia's brother, from Oregon to help him.

"We sent the telegram before we left Effingham," he said, "and we're awaitin' his answer, although I know he'll agree to the deal."

"Seth will be your foreman?" Sylvia cried, hardly daring to believe her ears. "You hadn't told me, Rory!"

"I knew it'd please you," he said, a grin breaking out on his face. "I instructed Seth to bring your mama, too." Turning to Lizzie and Brad, he explained, "Lizzie's brother lost his wife, 'n' he has two young'uns to raise."

Rory talked on, his face glowing with the admiration he felt for Sylvia's older brother, and Molly, who had been listening attentively in the background, felt a stirring of interest.

Seth Wyatt sounds like the kind of good man a woman dreams of meeting, she thought. Somehow, just the mention of his name struck an answering chord.

Then she tried to put aside further daydreams. What man would want a woman with a crooked leg? Besides, she was neither as handsome nor as smart as Mary Katharine, nor did she have Marissa's beauty and spirit. No, she'd do well to forget all about marryin'.

"Sylvia and Seth's mama's been helpin' him with the children, but she's gettin' older and tired. She could use some help." Rory glanced toward Molly, who still stood apart from the others. "I was just thinkin', Miss Molly, maybe you'd agree to hire on as their housekeeper to help Missus Wyatt with the young'uns—" He paused to gauge the effect of his words, then proceeded, "I can promise you, you'll be well-paid. And with room and board provided, you could put by a nice little nest egg."

"What a wonderful idea!" said Sylvia, her face alight. "And Seth's youngsters are so sweet and well-behaved."

Molly flushed under their scrutiny. "Well . . . I have no other plans—," she began hesitantly. "I suppose I could try . . . that is, if Mister Wyatt and his mother agree."

Rory was full of his plans. "I want to get the sawmill runnin' quick as we can. There's goin' to be a need for quality lumber with so many buildin's springin' up 'tween here 'n' town."

As Rory spoke on, Lizzie and Brad joined hands, their smiles dimming for only a moment as they saw Lester leave the barn, a cold and lonely youth as he bent into the bitter winter wind, burdened with a load too heavy to be borne alone.

In the warm pressure of their hands passed the silent knowledge that their son was not alone. He would discover, as they had, that the Lord was faithful. *He would not leave Lester without strength and hope to keep a straight course as he traverses through this world,* Lizzie thought.

Then her thoughts spun back to the berry patch where she'd found love again—at least, the promise of fulfillment in the Lord's own time. Looking around her now at her friends and family—the fruit of her life with Brad—she saw that their lush summer years were nearing a close. Soon it would be harvest time—a harvest ripe with hope. Without hope, how would they have made it through the trials?

Her gaze sought out and lingered on each of her children and Brad's—Thad and Harmony; Linda, Jayne, Patricia, and Rosalie; her brother Rory, Sylvia, and little Fanny Beth; Katie and Molly Wheeler. Ah, Molly—

There was a brave smile on the girl's face, though her heart must be sore. Lizzie had seen the sympathetic look that had followed Lester, a seeming soulmate in their shared loss over Marissa's departure. Was she the special one who would help him through his season of grief? Lizzie wondered. Or had he been so blinded by Marissa's gaiety and beguiling manner that he had overlooked Molly's more subtle beauty, her true worth?

Only time would tell.

And as one moment passed to become another, Lizzie lifted a prayer for this blessed family—every last one of them. Whatever the future held for Molly . . . for Marissa . . . for all of them, they could move on with faith and undiminished hope for the morrow—